Mostly, she watched him. It was an intense pleasure to feast her eyes on the harsh line of Brad's profile—the jut of his square chin, shadowed with evening stubble; the tousled mass of his dark hair; the strong arms that wielded the steering-wheel with such confident authority.

Tara wanted him. He had been right, she thought with quiet amusement, to make her wait. Yesterday she would willingly have made love with him, but today she knew him better, and she wanted him far more. By now she was almost sick with impatience to be in his arms. Every shared glance, every touch throughout that day had served to stoke her longing. And tonight, she felt sure, he would fulfil her every desire.

HEART IN FLAMES

BY

SALLY COOK

MILLS & BOON LIMITED
ETON HOUSE   18–24 PARADISE ROAD
RICHMOND   SURREY   TW9 1SR

*First published in Great Britain 1991
by Mills & Boon Limited*

© *Sally Cook 1991*

*Australian copyright 1991
Philippine copyright 1991
This edition 1991*

ISBN 0 263 77269 1

*Set in 10 on 11½ pt Linotron Times
01-9110-55741
Typeset in Great Britain by Centracet, Cambridge
Made and printed in Great Britain*

CHAPTER ONE

'YOU'RE sure you have to go on the roof?'

'I'm afraid so,' Tara Miller agreed.

'Then we take this ladder here. Ladies first—is that right?'

'Wrong, Jean-Claude,' Tara said with a grin. 'Since I'm wearing a skirt, it's perhaps as well if you *don't* follow me!'

Jean-Claude Morot, an easy-going mongrel of a man, shrugged and smiled. 'So why don't you wear trousers?'

'Insco's rules: always a smart suit, however dirty the work is, and always skirts for women.'

'Crazy.' He glanced down at his own practical dungarees, then back at her chocolate-brown two-piece, which would have been more suited to an accountant's office than a factory roof. It looked good on her, though, accentuating the neat but feminine lines of her figure. She had softened the severe cut by wearing with it a silky blouse with a pussycat bow, in a shade of dark lilac that added depth to the blue-grey of her eyes.

'You leave your papers here?' he asked.

'No, I'll bring them up. Then I'll be able to make notes if I want to—and it should be a good place to sketch the factory layout from.'

'That won't be easy, with the mistral blowing.'

'I'll pin the paper down,' she assured him. 'After you. . .'

'Sure,' Jean-Claude agreed, setting his hands on the slim metal ladder. Tara watched until he was around eight feet from the ground, then she began to climb

5

herself. She did so lithely and easily, the result of much practice. Her suit might look impractical, but she had chosen a style with a flaring skirt that didn't restrict her movements, and her shoes were flat-heeled and rubber-soled, providing a good grip on the narrow rungs.

She was breathing a little faster, but was far from exhausted when she reached the top of the tall building. Jean-Claude reached down to take her clipboard and papers, and she accepted his helping hand as she heaved herself up on to the roof, and paused to catch her breath and take her bearings.

The mistral wasn't strong today, but there was no shelter from it up here. It tugged at the ends of the curly fair hair which she wore caught up in a pony-tail, flicking them back against her face. A bright sun shone down from a cloudless sky. It was exhilarating to be out in the open, high up, the world at her feet. She accepted back her clipboard, then trailed Jean-Claude along a sequence of duck-boards that led to the edge of the gravelled expanse of roof.

From here they could see everything: the factory yard far below, the box-like buildings that made up the rest of the ECF complex, the cars parked in the car park and speeding along the straight road to Montelimar, and beyond, all around them, the blue-green hills that bordered the Rhône valley.

It was an attractive scene, even though there was nothing conventionally beautiful about the plastic-moulding factory. The noise of the pressing shop was dulled now to a faint thud and rumble, the air was clear, the chaos of the jumbled warehouse storage and the heaps of rubbish against the far end of the pressing shop were hidden from their view.

'So you see?' Jean-Claude said. 'Nothing here to burn.'

'The roof itself would,' Tara responded, raising her voice to combat the wind that carried it away from him. 'There's felt under the gravel, and I can't rule out the possibility of storm damage when the mistral's really blowing.'

'The roof's in good condition, surely?'

'Looks it, but there are tests I have to do to make sure. Tomorrow. There'll only be time to sketch the plan this afternoon.'

'So.' Jean-Claude came closer. 'Let me tell you what you see. Over there is the admin block—you came there when you arrived. To your left is the finished products warehouse, and there the raw materials warehouse, and—and there, in the yard, Monsieur Fillol himself. Oh, and. . .'

'Oh,' Tara echoed. Like Jean-Claude, she had recognised the figure of Monsieur Fillol—the dapper little general manager of the factory—emerging from the admin block and crossing the yard towards the pressing shop, on whose roof they stood. But she didn't recognise the man who had followed him out of the admin block, and who now walked beside him.

Whoever he was, he towered over Monsieur Fillol, moving with a rangy stride, as if most of his height consisted of leg. He wore a smart grey three-piece suit, and from the way Monsieur Fillol glanced nervously up at him every few seconds he had to be somebody important.

'That's Monsieur Hamilton. Sorry, Meester Hamilton,' Jean-Claude amended, with a sideways grin in acknowledgement that he was talking to an Englishwoman—even if her French was as good as his own. 'You've not met him?'

'No, I haven't. Who is he?'

'He's the—how you say in English?—"beeg cheese".'

'Managing director?'

'European director. You know ECF is part of SHP, the American group, now? Of course you do—that's why we have your American insurance company inspecting us. Mr Hamilton is the American who comes to tell us how to run our business.'

'And about time too,' Tara muttered, half under her breath.

'Not so loud.' Jean-Claude sounded amused rather than offended, but still he was serious in giving the warning. They might be standing thirty feet up, but Monsieur Fillol was approaching fast.

'So that's why Monsieur Fillol was too busy to talk to me,' Tara said thoughtfully, her eyes still on the American. Mr Hamilton. He hadn't been mentioned in her briefing notes, probably because he wasn't based at this ECF location. If she had known he was around she would have introduced herself earlier—and been more than glad to have a senior manager other than Fillol to deal with. Her initial poor impression of the general manager, who had been brusque and dismissive when she had arrived to do her insurance inspection, had been reinforced by the half-day she had already spent looking around his factory.

ECF's Montelimar factory had all the hallmarks of bad management: unhappy atmosphere, sloppy house-keeping, ill-informed staff. Even Jean-Claude—admittedly he was friendly and co-operative, but although his title of security manager sounded impressive Tara had already found out that he had only one man reporting to him, no budget control, and was hopelessly lacking in training for his job.

It would need more than a sheaf of recommendations

from her to put this location to rights; it needed a firm hand from above. Fillol clearly wasn't providing that, and Jean-Claude wasn't in a position to, so she had to rest her hopes on Mr Hamilton.

'He came yesterday,' Jean-Claude offered.

'Oh? And will he be here long?'

'Perhaps a month, perhaps more. He's careful not to say.'

A month? Sounded good. He'd not only be available to discuss her recommendations before she moved on, he would also have a chance to see them acted upon. What was more, Tara silently concluded, he would almost certainly be motivated to act upon them if he was a long-term employee of SHP. Insco had insured the huge American conglomerate for years, and had thoroughly indoctrinated its staff into the merits of their tough approach to fire protection.

'Does he have an office?' she asked thoughtfully.

'He's using the inteview-room. I'll show you later.'

'Thanks.'

'Now come back a little.' Jean-Claude caught her sleeve in his hand and tugged, pulling her away from the parapet.

'Why?'

'So they don't see you.'

'What's wrong with them seeing me? All right, I'm not burning to meet Monsieur Fillol again, but I'd be happy to let Mr Hamilton know I'm here.'

'I'd rather you didn't—*merde*!'

It was too late, because Monsieur Fillol had seen them—though in fact Mr Hamilton had done so first. His long stride-pattern had just snagged, then he had stopped, and moved back a couple of paces so that he could look up at them. He had caught Monsieur Fillol's sleeve and pointed upwards, and now the little manager was erupting in a torrent of gestures.

Presumably he was shouting something, too, since his mouth was opening and shutting, but the breeze was blowing his words away from them, leaving him looking like a particularly oily species of fish.

It didn't take much skill in reading mime to get the general drift, though.

'What's he got to be so upset about?' Tara asked exasperatedly.

'That you are still here, I suppose.'

'You could hardly have sent me away, Jean-Claude.'

'You try telling Monsieur Fillol that.'

'I will.' She turned and began to negotiate the way back across the roof to the ladder.

'Tara! Mademoiselle Miller! Wait. . .'

No, she wasn't waiting. She had made her own quick judgement of the situation, and she was going to act on it.

Problems like this happened so often that she got sick of them. Almost every factory manager trotted out the same old complaints. 'But you didn't tell us you were coming'—of course she didn't: half the point of insurance inspections was that they were unannounced, giving the inspector a chance to see the factory in precisely its normal condition. 'But you're a woman, and we don't like women in our factory.' Tough! *She* didn't like sex discrimination!

Acting apologetic got her nowhere, as she had discovered in her first few months on the job, so now she tended to take a forthright approach, mixed in with a little deviousness when necessary.

She suspected that, when Monsieur Fillol had passed her on so rapidly to Jean-Claude Morot, he had told the security manager to get rid of her—although she wasn't admitting that to either of them! If Mr Hamilton hadn't come on to the scene, she had planned to get her inspection completed behind Monsieur Fillol's back, and then march into his office at the end with her recommendations.

Now, though, she had a chance to take a different line. Mr Hamilton wasn't blind—he had surely seen all the signs of poor management that she herself had seen. A day into his own visit was the ideal time for him to start asserting his authority—and how better to do it than by giving her his public backing?

Jean-Claude was hurtling down the ladder as she reached the ground, but she didn't wait for him. She brushed down her skirt with her hand, tugged her jacket straight, tossed her pony-tail back, and strode towards the corner of the building.

She had barely reached it when Mr Hamilton and Monsieur Fillol rounded the corner and stopped short a pace away from her.

'Mr Hamilton, isn't it?' she asked in English. Smiling, brightly confident, she held out her hand. 'Tara Miller. I'm Insco's fire protection engineer, assigned to do an initial insurance inspection on this factory. I didn't know you were here, or I'd have introduced myself to you when I arrived, as well as to Monsieur Fillol here.'

She gave Monsieur Fillol the briefest of glances and smiles, not looking in his direction for long enough to give him a chance to register his anger with her, then turned back to the American.

Gosh, he was tall. She had seen from the roof that he overtopped Monsieur Fillol by quite a margin, but his figure had been foreshortened from that angle, and it hadn't really dawned on her how huge he was, or what he would be like to confront on the level.

Tara herself was a short woman, only five feet one, and in flat shoes her eyes barely came up to his chest. She had to crane her neck backwards to meet his gaze.

His breadth of shoulder matched his height, and in spite of the formal suit he had a rugged, outdoor look to him. Cowboy stock, she thought absently. She could imagine him in a Hollywood epic. He'd play the hero, of course. He wasn't conventionally handsome, but he was attractive—and more. Charismatic was the word for him. It wasn't just the size of him; he had the sort of presence that ensured that, in any company, he wouldn't be ignored.

He had a strong face, with just the faintest trace of stubble emphasising the harsh shape of his square jaw. His eyes were brown, set deep under thick level brows, and overhung by a heavy fringe of dark brown hair. As they latched on to hers she felt a sudden shock, as if he had physically touched her.

She had an urge to turn back to cheerful Jean-Claude, but she resisted it, though she drew back the hand he hadn't taken as unobtrusively as possible.

'You're a factory inspector?' he asked, in an incredulous voice.

'An insurance inspector, yes.' Tara's mouth was aching, but she kept up her broad smile and confident tone. 'I started my inspection this morning. I'm about to draw up a site plan, since you don't have a suitable one in your office, then tomorrow I'll go on to do my tests. It's hard to be specific, but I'm reckoning the inspection'll take two days in total. Perhaps I could grab this opportunity to fix an appointment with you for late Friday afternoon? I need to outline my recommendations before I leave—that's company policy.'

'That isn't a job for a woman.'

His accent wasn't the mid-west cowboy drawl she

had half expected: its taut twang indicated that he came from the north-east seaboard. His voice was deep and attractive—but his words certainly weren't!

'I can't agree with you there,' she said coldly.

'We don't allow women on our shop floor. Weren't you told that?'

Tara glared at him.

'A rule like that's not only discriminatory, Mr Hamilton—it's illegal. Surely you know that? It must be the same in the States. As an insurance inspector I've a contractual right to visit any part of your premises. You don't have any right to specify that Insco send a male inspector, just as they don't have any right to discriminate against employing women who are capable of doing the job. Which I am; I'm fully trained as a fire protection engineer.'

'Damn the feminist philosophy. Factories aren't any place for a woman.'

'Why? Do you imagine your workers are going to leap on me? I can assure you they won't! When I do get any trouble, it's invariably from managers, not from shop-floor operatives! The worst I suffer, going round a factory, is a few wolf-whistles and the odd glimpse of a "girlie" calendar!'

'She's a distraction to the men,' Monsieur Fillol put in, in a petulant voice. 'I told Morot to send her packing.'

'Then why's she still here?' Mr Hamilton demanded, turning to his general manager, and switching, like Fillol, to French—which he spoke fluently, though with a strong American accent.

'Perhaps he knows more about contract law then you do,' Tara said waspishly. 'Actually, Monsieur Morot's been the one helpful person I've met in this place.'

'Fillol,' Mr Hamilton went on, ignoring her as if she

hadn't spoken, 'I haven't time to waste on this kind of trivial matter. I'll leave it to you to make Miss Miller see sense. Come and join me in the packing shop as soon as you can.'

'I shan't go until I've finished my inspection,' Tara said heatedly.

'Monsieur Fillol will explain the situation to you,' Mr Hamilton curtly replied. 'Excuse me, Miss Miller.'

Excuse him! That was the last thing she felt like doing; in her book there weren't any excuses for his kind of aggressive unreasonableness! But she couldn't have physically held him back, and already he had half covered the distance to the packing shop in a series of long, loping strides.

Her eyes followed him. No wonder—he was the sort of man any woman would have turned to watch. But though that kind of forceful arrogance went down a treat on the cinema screen, it didn't please her at all in real life. He was just the sort of chauvinistic male she most destested.

He disappeared round the corner of the finished goods warehouse, and Tara wrenched her eyes back to Monsieur Fillol—to find, unsurprisingly, that he was furious.

His anger wasn't directed at her, though, but at Jean-Claude, who had been lingering by the wall of the pressing shop.

'Look what you've done now, Morot,' he spat out.

'I told her to keep away from Hamilton,' Jean-Claude said, with a shrug.

'Away from Hamilton? That's not all I told you! I told you to get her off the premises.'

'No can do, Monsieur Fillol. She showed me the insurance conditions. She's right, she has the authority to do her inspection.'

'What authority? Let me tell you, *I* am the authority in this factory, and I don't like insubordination!'

'I was only doing what I thought——'

'Think!' screeched the little Frenchman. 'You never think! That's your trouble, Morot, you're a blockhead! I've had enough of your stupid behaviour. You're fired right now. Get your things and get out. As for you, miss, you can follow him.'

'That's ridiculous,' Tara exclaimed. 'You can't fire a man just like that. Anyway, Monsieur Morot's right. I'm legally authorised to carry out my inspection, and that's what I'll be doing.'

'You get out right now before you make any more trouble. And tell your boss to send a man to do a man's job next time! Morot, see her off the premises right away.'

Monsieur Fillol glared at them both for a moment more, then pursed his lips as if he was tempted to spit, and marched off with Napoleonic arrogance.

'*Merde*,' Jean-Claude muttered.

'*Merde*, indeed,' Tara agreed.

'Why is it a woman has to do your job?'

'Just because women get reactions like that, Jean-Claude. We can't let men get away with it, so we have to persevere. We're pioneers, and we have it tough, but it's worth it for the sake of the women who come after us.'

'Worth losing me my job?'

'He surely can't have meant that.'

'You want to bet?' Jean-Claude's normally cheerful face drooped. 'Fillol's the sort of man who always acts before he thinks, and never goes back on it, even when he realises he's made a mistake. And to fire me. . .it couldn't come at a worse time. Last week my car breaks down, Saturday I commit myself to buying a new one, and today I lose my job.'

'Oh, Jean-Claude, I'm so sorry. There must be something we can do. All right, maybe it's no use pleading with Fillol, but surely Mr Hamilton didn't mean that to happen. Perhaps you should talk to him. . .'

'Hah! Mr Hamilton! Yesterday I go to him, and Henri Sarlat too, and we tell him that Fillol is a corrupt fool. We say, "You must get rid of this man," and what does he say? That he waits and sees for himself! I tell you, that man will do nothing.'

'It's worth a try, surely.'

'Pssch! I fight Fillol, sure, but not like that.'

'Then I'll go and talk to Mr Hamilton.'

'But you are to leave now—you heard Fillol say so.'

'So I did.' Tara gave Jean-Claude her sweetest smile. 'But since you're not his employee any more, there's no reason for you to carry out his orders, is there, Jean-Claude?'

A flicker of hope lit up Jean-Claude's eyes.

'You would go? You would talk to him for me?'

'Sure—and for me too. I've no intention of giving up my inspection halfway through. I'll keep out of Fillol's way, but I'll certainly have another go at making Hamilton see sense.'

'There's a back way to the admin block, so you can get there without passing Fillol's office window. I show you now. . .?'

'Lead the way.'

It was no surprise to Tara or to Jean-Claude when they found that the interview-room, which Mr Hamilton was using as an office, was empty—after all, they had just seen him going off in the opposite direction. The door was unlocked, though, and Tara assured Jean-Claude that she would wait there until Mr Hamilton returned.

'What if Monsieur Fillol comes in with him?' Jean-Claude asked dubiously.

'I'll deal with it, don't worry. I promise you, I'll do all that I can.'

'It's three o'clock now. I go get my things together. You'll be all right?'

'I'll be fine. And, Jean-Claude—good luck.'

'It is you who needs that, I think.' Jean-Claude managed a very French smile of appreciation, then he stood aside to let Tara into the room, and closed the door after her.

She glanced around her, realised that her eyes had automatically moved upwards to search for sprinklers in the ceiling, and snorted with laughter. She was as thoroughly conditioned as a homing-pigeon! Still, it was reassuring to see that the sprinklers were there. The basic fire precautions in this factory looked to be good; it was just the housekeeping standards that were atrocious.

So it wouldn't cost much to set the place to rights— but getting that done might still not be easy, she thought to herself. Insco's powers were limited. They could threaten to raise premiums, or as a last resort they could cancel a client's insurance; but they couldn't compel their clients to carry out improvements in the same way that they could compel them to allow inspections.

Badly kept, badly protected factories angered Tara. Some managers thought purely in cost terms—how many years of reduced premiums it would take to pay for a fire pump or a hydrant—but really that wasn't the issue, she believed. They didn't consider the disruption, the unfulfilled orders, the sheer *waste* that a major fire caused. Those things couldn't easily be quantified, but Insco wasn't in business to insure those who didn't appreciate them.

It would be surprising if Mr Hamilton didn't appreciate them, she thought. An American who had been appointed European Manager, he must have worked for SHP for years. It only made sense to assume that he had absorbed the company philosophy that had led them to choose Insco as an insurer.

But then, it had made sense to assume that he had accepted modern attitudes to women doing traditionally male jobs, and she had certainly been wrong there!

Why had he been so antagonistic? She couldn't understand it. Even if he didn't like to see women in his factories, there had been no need to be so aggressive in telling her so. In her book, good management consisted of gently persuading people to do as you wanted, not of bossing them around!

To be fair, though, she hadn't handled the situation particularly well herself, she thought ruefully. Mr Hamilton had had an unnerving effect on her. She'd risen too quickly to his bait, when she would have done better to use her feminine charms on him.

After all, if a woman had to put up with the disadvantages of being female, it was only fair if she used the advantages too!

She crossed the room, which was drably painted in cream and sparsely furnished, and looked at the table Mr Hamilton was using as a desk. There were only a few papers on it: an internal telephone list, a list of the employee names and functions, and an unused notepad. No wonder he hadn't bothered to lock his room—even the most inventive industrial spy wouldn't find anything interesting there.

Nothing to read; nothing to do. She perched on the edge of the desk and looked out of the window. All she could see were a couple of spindly poplars, bent over by the force of the mistral, and the wall of the finishing shop.

She set her briefcase down on the table, opened it, and extracted a comb and pocket mirror. She would feel more confident, *and* have more chance of charming him, if she looked her best when Mr Hamilton appeared—and her hair had suffered from the wind on the roof. She pulled off the fastening that held it back, combed it through, listening out all the time for footsteps, and refastened it.

She renewed her deep-pink lipstick, and smiled into the mirror. She looked all right—in fact, better than all right. It wasn't Tara's style to spend hours on her appearance, but fortunately nature had blessed her with a perfect oval face, flawless skin and good features, so she didn't need to work particularly hard in order to appear attractive.

For Monsieur Fillol, who that morning had pinched her bottom before telling her to run along, she wouldn't have spared a scrap of lipstick; but for Mr Hamilton she would. Not because she liked him—in fact, she was well on the way to detesting him—but because she knew that the current of attraction running between them might prove useful to her.

Where was he, anyway? She glanced at her watch. It was barely ten past three. He might not come back to his office for an hour or more, she thought pragmatically.

There was an empty table in the corner of the room, so she carried her briefcase over to that, sat down, and got out her notepad. She couldn't afford to waste any more time, since her schedule was tight, and while she was waiting she would be able to jot down some notes for her report, and do a rough sketch of what she remembered of the factory layout.

Soon she became absorbed in the work, and forgot to keep listening out. The clunk of the door opening made her start in surprise.

Mr Hamilton strode in, heading straight for his desk. He picked up the telephone, sat on the edge of the desk just as Tara had done, pulled a pen out of his jacket pocket and drew the notepad towards him.

His back was towards her, and he hadn't noticed her sitting in the corner. 'Get me Carson in Boston,' he barked into the telephone.

'Perhaps we should talk first,' Tara said quietly.

Mr Hamilton jumped, swung round, and dropped the telephone, all in the same movement.

'Sorry if I scared you.' She rose to her feet. Now that he was here, she felt a little nervous about her mission, and she hesitated to go any closer to him. He looked big enough even at six-foot range! 'I just thought you might prefer not to make your phone-call while I'm here,' she finished limply.

'What the hell are you doing here?'

'I need to talk to you.' She took a deep breath. 'You ought to know straight away that as soon as you left Fillol this afternoon he not only told me to leave the factory, he also fired Jean-Claude Morot.'

'Fired him?'

'Just like that.' She snapped her fingers. 'In front of me.'

Silence. Mr Hamilton's eyes narrowed, and he met her challenging stare head-on. Tara met it back the same way. Nervous or not, she had committed herself now.

She didn't have to stare him out, though, because it

was he who quickly dropped his eyes. He bent to replace the telephone on its rest, then slid to his feet, thrust his hands in his pockets, and strode towards the window. His eyes on the puny poplars, he said slowly, 'I see. I guess I owe you an apology for the embarrassment you've been caused.'

'I guess you do, but that's not why I came. I came to ask you to reinstate Monsieur Morot.'

'You what!' Mr Hamilton demanded, spinning round to confront her again.

Tara's exasperation rose. Did he have to react as if she was being petulant and unreasonable? 'For heaven's sake,' she said heatedly, 'you must realise that Fillol's as weak as he is incompetent. You only have to look around this factory to see that it's atrociously run. I spent several hours with Monsieur Morot today, and I can assure you that he's a good security manager— under-trained, but intelligent and willing. He didn't deserve to be fired, and in my opinion it was one of the most petty and spiteful acts I've ever witnessed. Fillol was just looking for the nearest scapegoat, and you can't allow him to get away with that sort of behaviour.'

'Do you think this is any of your business, Miss Miller?'

'Certainly I do. I don't think anyone ought to stand by and watch somebody being victimised without speaking up about it.'

'Perhaps I should remind you that you're not an employee of this company.'

'That's just as well. I wouldn't work for any company as badly run as this one.'

'Miss Miller, I think you'd better leave.'

This was said in a thoroughly forbidding tone, and Mr Hamilton took a step towards her as he spoke. Inwardly, Tara quailed. It wasn't fair that he should use his size and strength to intimidate her—but he was doing so, and it did!

She wasn't giving in so easily, though.

'I'll go when I've got your assurance that you'll do something about this.'

'My God, you're a little spitfire, aren't you?'

'A *what*?' Sheer fury made Tara forget her unease, as she moved forward to confront him. 'You—you *chauvinist*! Now you just stop and think what a man would do in my situation! I came here to do a job that I've every right to do. First I'm patronised by the management, then I'm insulted, and then I see a man fired—and for what? For the *crime* of helping me do my job! Finally, I'm ordered to leave! What am I supposed to do? Take my medicine meekly and go crawling back to my boss? I can tell you, if I go back to my boss it won't be to ask him to send a man in my place! It'll be to send a complaint to the chairman of SHP, and to have this plant's insurance cancelled immediately for breach of contract!'

For a moment, through the red haze of her fury, she sensed that Mr Hamilton too was at the very brink of his self-control. His huge body seemed to swell within his elegant suit. His brows lowered, and he bore a distinctly unfunny resemblance to a bull about to charge. Then he seemed to recover himself, the moment of danger was past, and it was in a cold, controlled voice that he said, 'Just stop the hysterics.'

'Hysterics? Hysterics! This isn't hysterics, Mr Hamilton, this is justified fury!'

'All right, it's fury. Now cool it, please.'

'Listen to me sensibly and I will,' Tara retorted.

'I've heard you. And I give you my word I'll investigate the information you've given me.'

'That's not good enough. I want your word that you'll reinstate Morot.'

'Well, you can't have it.' Mr Hamilton took a deep breath. His eyes connected with hers for an instant, and a strange surge of awareness connected them. Then once again he broke the contact, turning his back on her as he strode back to his desk.

He set his hands on the metal desk-top, leaned forward, and said flatly, 'Be reasonable, Miss Miller. You can't expect me to make that kind of commitment without investigating for myself. I've only your word for what happened—I need to hear Morot's version, and Fillol's, before I can take any action. I've told you I'll do that, and I will, but I sure as hell won't promise what action I'm going to take. You're not the manager of this factory. And to tell the truth, I think you're extremely unwise if you make a habit of interfering with the internal affairs of client companies.'

'I don't,' she assured him. That was true, as a rule—all Insco's inspectors had it drummed into them that they shouldn't do so, and she was uneasily conscious that she hadn't exactly been the soul of discretion.

'I'm glad to hear it.'

'I'm still waiting for you to clear the way for me to finish my inspection.'

Mr Hamilton sighed.

'I've a right to complete it,' Tara reminded him.

'Yeah, I guess you have.' He straightened up, and looked at her again. 'But I don't want you doing it.'

'Well, frankly, I don't care what you want, Mr Hamilton!'

'I dare say you don't, but I'm telling you anyway. I know I'm legally in the wrong, and I shouldn't have spoken to you the way I did in the yard—but I don't want you in my factory.'

'And what do you think would happen if I backed down in front of every male chauvinist who grumbled that I was distracting his employees? I can tell you! I'd be out of a job even faster than Jean-Claude was!'

'I'm not trying to make trouble for you. I'll phone your boss and clear it with him.'

'Will you hell!' Tara swept her papers back into her briefcase and shut it with an emphatic click. 'I'll be back in the morning to inspect your factory, Mr Hamilton. If I have to I'll go to my boss, to your boss, I'll even call in the *gendarmes*. But you bet I'll be here!'

She picked up her briefcase and strode towards the door. At least, a step towards it—which was all she could manage without running slap bang into Mr Hamilton, who was standing in front of it.

'Excuse *me*,' she said icily.

'For God's sake, woman! How am I supposed to trust my employees with you around?'

'If anyone tries anything on me, you'll soon find out I know how to protect myself!'

'Do you?' He reached out and put a hand on her shoulder.

A shiver ran right through Tara's slight body.

'Don't you. . .' she faltered.

But Mr Hamilton wasn't listening. A second hand followed the first, and together they pulled her inexorably towards him. Before she could frame a protest, his mouth slammed down on hers.

His kiss held all the anger he'd held in during their confrontation, unleashed in an explosion of raw power. For an instant Tara froze. Then emotion rushed in—a hot, intense rush of it that seared through her body like a gas explosion. She couldn't have said if she was punishing him or desiring him—there only came, terrifyingly, the realisation that she was kissing him back.

No sooner had it come than it led to a reflex urge for escape. Gathering her force, she pushed against the solid wall of his chest, tore her mouth away from the bruising pressure of his. He let her go instantly, and for a moment they stood there, shaking. Then Tara urged her legs into action, and fled from the room.

She hurtled down the corridor, pushed through the door at the other end, and subsided against the outside wall of the admin block.

The shaking was back, so fierce that she could barely believe she'd found the strength to escape him. Warily, she glanced back at the door, but it stayed shut behind her.

No, he wouldn't come. He wasn't insane, he'd had a moment to come to his senses, and he must realise that that added up to sexual harassment of the very worst kind.

She'd faced a few sticky situations before—didn't every pretty woman who worked with men?—but never anything like that. The sheer power of him! She hadn't been boasting when she'd claimed she could look after herself, having got the better of quite a few men who had tried to take advantage of her slightness, but somehow that man had disarmed her completely.

It hadn't been physical strength, though he wasn't lacking in that; it was something else, something much more disturbing. For the first time in her working life she felt afraid—but not so much of Mr Hamilton, as of herself.

How could she have been so weak? Running away! She should have kneed him where it would hurt, screamed rape, attacked him with her sarcasm. And what had she done? Run!

She regretted it; she hated knowing she'd done it. But she couldn't find it in herself to go back through that door and confront Mr Hamilton again. All she wanted was to get away, a million miles away from him.

But her job. . .?

She didn't want to back down and give up the inspection, but she had to be reasonable, and accept her own limitations. She was badly shaken by the incident, and needed time to recover—and nor could she realistically get on with the inspection now that she had lost her guide. The factory site was confusingly laid out, and though its plastic-moulding activities weren't particularly dangerous, it wouldn't have done for an ignorant outsider to wander around unsupervised.

Anyway, it was past four o'clock, and she had risen at six that morning to drive to Montelimar from her previous assignment near Lyons. The logical answer was to give up and go back to her hotel. That would give her time to recover, to sleep on the problem, and then she would be able to decide what to do next in the morning.

She picked up the briefcase that she'd dropped on the ground, and tried to look casual and composed as she walked to the factory car park.

The little Fiat which she had hired in Lyons was parked next to a gleaming red Ferrari—a new one, too. No prizes for guessing who that belonged to, she thought sarcastically. That was a male chauvinist's car if ever there was one!

It was a rich man's car, also, and a young man's car. How apt—Mr Hamilton was young for a man in his position—not more than thirty-five, she guessed—and doubtless very well paid, as European director of a huge corporation. All in all, not the best man to make an enemy of, as her boss Jim Backley would doubtless tell her, she thought ruefully.

There had to be at least a dozen ECF factories and warehouses in France, and Insco needed to inspect them all. She had been expecting to do a lot of that work herself, but now she would have to try to talk Jim into assigning it to somebody else. Damn Mr Hamilton. Self-assured she might be, but she couldn't handle him, and she knew it.

It was a relief to return her site pass to the guard on the gate, and to know that, until the morning at least, she was free of him. It was only a fifteen-minute drive to the centre of Montelimar and the smallish but very pleasant hotel she had checked in to that morning, and then she was able to relax properly—showering, changing, and watching an hour of the early-evening television.

A good supper, an early night and she'd feel almost her usual self, she thought, as she made her way down to the hotel dining-room. Then, in the morning, she planned to make one more attempt to complete her inspection, withdrawing at the first hint of trouble. If Fillol and Hamilton didn't change their tune, she'd just have to phone Jim, and take his advice on how to handle the situation.

'Ah *mademoiselle*,' the head waiter greeted her. 'Your room number? You eat alone?'

'Yes, I'm alone. Room twenty-three. Could I have a corner table, perhaps?'

'Sit where you choose, *mademoiselle*. It's early, we are not busy yet.'

She followed his gesturing hand into the plushly furnished dining-room, and glanced around.

He had told the truth: there were only a dozen customers in the room. One of them, sitting alone at a table by the window, was Mr Hamilton.

CHAPTER TWO

OH, NO! Tara thought, horrified, as she stepped back, searching instinctively for somewhere to hide from him. She couldn't face him watching her over dinner—she'd just have to go and find somewhere else to eat.

Before she had a chance to retreat, though, Mr Hamilton glanced up from the menu he had been studying.

He saw her immediately, and she didn't think to look away in time, so their eyes connected in a bright flash of tension. Slowly he rose to his feet.

Tara gave him a curt nod. Curse it, she couldn't leave now, not if she planned to confront him again in the morning. He'd take it as evidence that she was scared of him, and that would destroy her last chance of getting the better of him.

Quickly, she walked towards a small table at the far side of the room. She reached it, set her hand on the back of the nearest chair—and found Mr Hamilton's hand firmly descending on the other side of the chair-back.

'We can hardly ignore each other,' he said. 'Come and eat with me.'

'No, thank you,' she stiffly replied. 'I'd rather be alone.'

'And I'm the last man you wanted to see, I guess.' He gave her a rueful smile. 'Not that I blame you—but being alone is the last thing I want, right now. To tell the truth, I'm sick of evenings alone—sick of speaking French all the time, too. We'd have to patch things up when you come back to the plant in the morning, so we might as well do it now. Please?'

Tara had opened her mouth to give him a tart retort, but by the time he reached the end of this speech she had thought better of it. A moment's thought, then, 'Does that mean you'll clear the path for my inspection?' she asked warily.

'Haven't any damn choice, have I?'

'No,' she quickly agreed.

'OK, then. Come and join me.'

She hesitated before replying. It would make sense, she supposed, to be pleasant to him, but she wasn't sure she could bring herself to do it. How was she supposed to make polite conversation for a couple of hours, when she hated everything he stood for, and the air around them was humming with a heady mixture of sexuality and resentment? Being in his company was like putting a naked flame near a gas jet. Relations between them might be rocky already, but she could think of one or two ways in which they could become a whole lot worse.

'I want to make this clear,' she said slowly. 'This is strictly business, right?'

'Wrong,' Mr Hamilton said, in a quiet but firm voice. 'A man and a woman together aren't ever strictly business—not us two, leastways. You don't have to eat with me in order to get back into the factory—I've already told you I'll go along with that. I don't want to talk insurance, I'm asking you because I want to spend this evening with you. And I do mean this evening, not tonight as well.'

'I should hope not!'

'Should you?' He reached out and took her arm, easing her grip from the chair-back and guiding her across the restaurant to his window-table.

His touch was like an electric shock to her. What was more, he knew it, she thought uncomfortably. It might be insufferably arrogant of him to spell it out that she was attracted to him, but she couldn't honestly dispute it.

Still, another comment like that and she would have turned tail, and to hell with hatchet-burying. So it was just as well for Mr Hamilton that there wasn't anything more she could object to in his manner or words as he pulled out a chair for her, reclaimed his own chair opposite, and offered her a drink.

She asked for a dry Martini, then had a minute's respite while he attracted the waiter's attention and ordered it.

Like her, he'd changed for the evening, into fawn trousers and a multi-coloured striped shirt, which he wore with sleeves rolled up and neck open. He looked younger out of his formal work clothes—or was it the different setting that gave her that impression?

Her eyes lingered on the firm clean line of his jaw. He'd shaved too, and showered—his hair was still darkened by damp. She took in the muscularity of his exposed forearms, couldn't help recalling his touch that afternoon, and felt her stomach muscles contract involuntarily.

Her tongue moistened the lips that were still swollen from his kiss. Harassment, that was what it had been. But this man surely didn't need to use coercion to get women into his bed. He had it all: power, money and raw male sexuality.

'It's Tara, isn't it? And I'm Brad.'

'Short for Bradley?' She seized eagerly on the casual topic of conversation that he offered.

'No, short for Bradford, Yorkshire. It's where my ancestors are supposed to have come from.'

'That's a strange place to name somebody after. It's not the most romantic of towns.'

'Maybe, but my American mother wasn't to know that.' He smiled, a wide, white, very attractive smile which Tara found herself responding to, in spite of all her wariness. 'Bradford's not so bad. I spent a weekend there a couple of years ago. You're not from round there, I guess? You're from southern England?'

'No, the Midlands—near Coventry.'

'Ah. I'm not so hot on English accents.'

Silence.

'What I can't understand,' Brad said suddenly, 'is why a woman like you should even want to do a job like yours.'

'Can't you?' Tara's tension came out in the way she almost spat her words at him. 'Then you must be very narrow-minded. What kind of job do you think I ought to do? Typing or nursing, I suppose?'

'What's wrong with that?'

'Nothing, for the right people—which I'm not. I never wanted a badly paid, dead-end job.'

'Those don't have to be dead-end jobs. Other women's jobs aren't. You could be a model, say.'

'You must be joking!'

'Why? You're beautiful—you know that. You might not make much of it, but it's all there.'

'By "it", you mean sex appeal, I suppose. Well, if I went swanning around your factory in hot-pants and a tight T-shirt, you really would have something to complain about!'

'No need to exaggerate,' Brad said sharply. 'Anyway, that's my point. You've chosen a job where you can't make the most of yourself, and I don't see why.'

'Maybe because it has other merits,' Tara retorted.

'There are more ways of making the most of yourself than attracting the opposite sex! There are better jobs than standing around letting people take photographs of you. My job's well paid. I get to travel worldwide, to see people and places I wouldn't see otherwise. It's always interesting. Some people reckon insurance is dull, and maybe they're right, but there's nothing dull about fire, or water either. I've seen Insco's fire tests on stacks of finished-goods storage like yours at ECF, and when I look in those warehouses I can picture the enemy, see the flames licking round the boxes, up to the ceiling, and the water showering down to fight them. Even to hold a fire hose in your hands and feel it buck with the pressure—ever done that?' she challenged suddenly.

'I can't say I have.'

'Then you should, and maybe you'd understand.'

Brad slowly shook his head. 'That side I might understand, but not the rest of it. A woman like you isn't safe in a factory.'

'Not from men like you, certainly!'

She saw his lips tighten. 'OK,' he said evenly, 'maybe I deserved that. All the same, I can't see how any boyfriend of yours could stand it, knowing you're the only woman among men all day. I can't see why you'd want the sort of man who'd let you do that kind of job.'

'Maybe,' Tara said tightly, 'I don't want any man at all.'

'I don't believe you.'

'It's true.' She shrugged. 'I'm not the marrying kind—I like my privacy. I like being free to travel, and I don't like being bossed around by men who kid themselves they're protecting me.'

'So you don't have a boyfriend.'

'Nor do I want one. My job isn't the kind that goes with a stable home life.'

'Everyone needs someone, though.'

'Speak for yourself!'

'I can hardly do that—I've been divorced nearly ten years.'

'Oh, and I pictured you married to some happy homebird who'll sit on her nest all day and never complain!'

'Did you?' He smiled again, lazily, tauntingly, as if he reckoned she'd pictured him quite differently. Which, to be honest, she had, but she didn't like the idea that he could read her thoughts quite that easily. So it was a relief to her when the waiter reappeared, and they had to drop the conversation in favour of choosing their supper.

A pleasure it was, too, since they were in a region renowned for its good food, and in a restaurant that offered the best of it. They both settled on *pâté en croûte* followed by *faux-filet*, and, after a long discussion with the wine-waiter, Brad ordered a bottle of Crozes-Hermitage.

'You know a lot about French wine,' Tara commented when the waiter had gone.

'Quite a bit. I'm fond of wine.'

'And of France? Have you been here long?'

'Four months, this time—since SHP started negotiations to take over ECF.'

'This time? So you've lived here before?'

'Years ago,' he answered offhandedly.

'When? Where?'

'It doesn't matter.'

No, it didn't *matter*, but it interested her. He might read her easily, but she couldn't yet understand him. Somehow he wasn't like most of the successful men she'd met, but she couldn't put her finger on how, or why.

Nor did Brad seem inclined to tell her. Now they'd aired their issues of contention, their conversation settled into an easier groove, but Tara was conscious that he was steering it the way he chose the whole time.

He talked a little about ECF, explaining that one reason he hadn't wanted her to do her inspection was because he had feared she would inflame the troubles at the plant. Though he hadn't acted to resolve the situation yet, she soon realised that he shared Jean-Claude's low opinion of Fillol. Confidentially, he admitted to her that Montelimar stood out as the plant in the ECF group with the worst results, which was why he had chosen to investigate it in depth so soon after taking over.

While he was frank about this, though, she couldn't push him on his private life. He clammed up as soon as she referred again to the divorce he'd mentioned, didn't show any inclination to talk about his previous stay in France, and didn't talk much about his life in the States either.

Instead he talked about impersonal subjects: wine, food, the French cinema, French politics. Although he'd risen high and fast in SHP, he clearly wasn't the obsessed, workaholic type. He had a wide range of interests, and Tara enjoyed their conversation. She might not like some of Brad's attitudes, but they seemed to have a great deal in common in other directions.

The evening that she had expected to be an ordeal turned imperceptibly into a pleasure. And maybe that wasn't such a surprise, because if she were honest she often did find it lonely, travelling from town to town, a stranger everywhere—and often an unwelcome one.

There were so few evenings when she had the chance to 'touch base' with somebody. Admittedly Brad wasn't the most likely of soul mates, but, strangely, the fact that they'd started off on such a bad footing had helped to break the ice. She didn't feel the need to be as reserved and polite with him as she usually was with clients. Soon they found themselves arguing again—over a film he'd liked and she hadn't, a politician she admired and he didn't—but it was more like the amicable bickering of good friends this time, easily dissolved in laughter.

The black southern night began to fall on the small French town, and still they sat at the window-table, eating brie and drinking brandy and black coffee. The restaurant began to empty, but Tara didn't want to break the spell, and go up to her lonely room.

'More coffee?' the waiter asked.

'We must have had three cups,' Brad answered, with a glancing smile at Tara, as if it surprised him, too, that they had got on so well. 'The bill goes on my account. Hey,' he went on to Tara, 'it's not so late—it's barely ten o'clock. Come for a walk around the town?'

Tara hesitated. Did he mean a walk, literally? Could she trust him? Could she trust herself? She wasn't tired, and she liked the idea of staying with him for a little longer, but she didn't want to give him the wrong kind of green light.

'Just a walk,' Brad persisted. 'Ten, fifteen minutes.'

Oh, why not? It didn't feel as if the evening was over yet. She felt restless—she wanted something else, something more, to happen.

'OK.'

They fetched jackets from their rooms, since the air was now cool, and met up by the reception desk. Then they set off, side by side, down the narrow, darkening streets of Montelimar.

Tara wouldn't have left the hotel after dark on her own. The town was quiet, and a little eerie. But at Brad's suggestion they kept to the brightly lit shopping centre, and she felt quite safe with his huge bulk by her side.

There was no moon, but the stars were bright, and they stopped several times when they were out of range of the neon lights, to gaze up at them.

Montelimar was 'nougat town', the French centre of production for the chewy sweet. They passed first one nougat shop, then another, and then another.

Soft nougat, hard nougat, nougat with nuts, nougat with preserved fruits, chocolate-flavoured nougat—every possible variation was on sale, in every size from small slabs to vast gift boxes costing a small fortune. There were dozens of shops selling it, tons of nougat, lorry-loads of the stuff.

'It's tourist trade,' Brad explained.

'So much of it? This isn't a tourist town, surely?'

'It's not Michelin-starred, but you have to pass by here if you're taking the main autoroute south to the Côte d'Azur. Quite a few tourists stop off, I guess, to buy nougat.'

'Fancy making a detour just for sweets,' Tara said with a laugh. 'I wonder if we insure nougat factories?'

'They can't be much of a fire risk.'

'You'd be surprised. Some people think that of plastics factories, though in fact they're among the most dangerous of all. Almost every trade has its hazards. Nougat factories must have ovens, and supplies of sugar—that's tricky stuff—and stacks of cardboard boxes, and walls, and roofs, and. . .actually many of them are probably little back-street workshops, and those can be really lethal.'

He smiled at the enthusiasm in her voice. 'Lethal—that's a powerful word.'

'It's a powerful subject.'

'To you, maybe.'

'It should be a vital subject to everyone. It really annoys me when factory managers act as if fire protection isn't important. Did you know that even when they're fully insured, most factories that have really bad fires never restart production again?'

'Maybe; but it can't happen that often.'

'Often enough.' She came to a halt in the street, and gazed earnestly at him. 'You've got to understand that, Brad. My job might be a joke to you, but the fires I help prevent are no joke. You've got to take my recommendations very seriously.'

'I will.'

They were just approaching a small square which sloped downhill from the road they had been walking along. Along the near side, the bright windows of shops shone out their bland message, while along the far side there loomed the dark shape of a large church. There was nobody else in sight—they might have been alone in the whole world.

'Tara,' Brad said, more gently, 'don't misunderstand me. I don't doubt you're good at your job. I wasn't trying to stop you doing your inspection because I'm the kind of man who believes women can't do technical work. It was just—seeing you, your small figure, on that roof-top really got to me. You looked so vulnerable. And some of the comments Fillol made—you didn't hear them, but I can tell you, they were pretty rich. I didn't want you exposed to that kind of thing. I just had an urge to protect you—and OK, I went a damn silly way about doing it.'

'I don't want that kind of protection,' Tara said defensively.

'But I want to give it to you.' He reached out and touched her hair with his hand, then let his fingers drift down the line of her neck; then caught her more firmly by the shoulder, and pulled her to him.

He held her close, pinned against the broad expanse of his chest. 'Dammit,' he murmured, bending his head to hers, 'I don't trust myself with you, so how am I to trust other men?'

'It's not them, it's me you have to trust,' Tara whispered back. Her mind was in a whirl. She couldn't help responding to his nearness. She couldn't help enjoying the feel of his big body enveloping hers. It did feel as if she was being protected, and a part of her liked that feeling, but a part of her reacted almost with fear, as if he was trying to trap her and she needed to get away.

'You're not as strong as you think you are,' Brad said softly. 'You're so small, so fragile.' His hands traced the slender curves of her body. 'Let me look after you.'

Hypnotised by his movements, by the intense look in his dark eyes, Tara didn't make any reply. There was a timeless moment when they stood there, bodies touching; then his lips touched hers.

The kiss started out gentle, but it soon changed. It held desire, raw hunger, her own confusion and uncertainty—and, far beneath that, a plain clear conviction that this was the right thing for them both. Tara's mouth opened, her tongue moved forward to meet his, and her body strained upwards and forwards, intensifying the contact between them. She wanted this, wanted his strength and his certainty and even his male arrogance, wanted it to match and complete her.

'I want you,' Brad breathed. 'I want you now. Let's go back now.'

'Brad. . .' She didn't want to go back, she wanted this to go on and on. She wanted to stay here, in the street, being held by him, kissing him.

'You want it too,' Brad whispered insistently. 'Don't you? I can feel you do. Come on, let's go and make love.'

'Brad!' The exclamation, and the abrupt movement that had her pushing him away, jerking back from him, came at the same instant. She gulped air, as if she was surfacing from too long spent underwater.

'Tara. . .?'

'No,' she said vehemently. 'No, I. . . I don't want that.'

'You could sure have fooled me.'

She flushed deeply, and turned away from him. But he came after her, catching her arm as she set off rapidly down the street.

'Tara, what's wrong? What did I say? What did I do? Tell me, please, because I sure as hell don't know.'

'It's not what you said!' She stopped abruptly, shaking her arm free from his restraining hand. 'It's this—our situation—everything.'

'I don't understand.'

'You must understand! For heaven's sake, tomorrow evening I'll be gone from here!'

'So? We've tonight, haven't we? And tomorrow? And the weekend—do you have to be anywhere particular for the weekend?'

'No. Well—I planned to go to Arles, but that's not. . . But it's not enough, Brad. I don't do this kind of thing. One-night stands, weekends with strangers— I don't want that kind of life.'

'I wasn't reckoning you did it all the time,' Brad

growled. 'It's not like that between us, and don't you make out that it is. This is special. Maybe it can't last for long, but it's still special. There's no one else, you said, so you haven't any reason not to.'

'It's enough of a reason that I'll be moving on.'

'Not to me it isn't. Tara, you can't pass up on relationships altogether. All right, you're not in a position to have a lasting relationship—so what's wrong with enjoying the ones that you can have?'

'Brad, I can't act like that. I don't trust myself to stay uninvolved. If I did spend the night with you on your terms, it wouldn't be worth it, and I might just be whetting my appetite for something I can't have.'

'You're sure?'

'Very sure.'

He sighed. 'I won't push you to do anything you don't want to do, but I sure can't help feeling that's a lonely way to live your life.'

'Maybe it is,' Tara said tightly, 'but it's my way.'

They retraced their steps to the hotel in silence. As soon as they arrived Brad said a brusque, 'Goodnight,' and hurried off, leaving Tara to climb the stairs to her room alone.

It was a pleasant room, but there was something about the sight of her solitary suitcase sitting open on the bed that brought out in her an acute feeling of desolation.

So what? It was only self-pity, and how she hated that! Nobody's life was perfect, and everybody occasionally had tough decisions to make. All right, her job was lonely, but it provided plenty of compensations. That evening, even—it had been such an enjoyable evening, until Brad had spoiled it by asking for more than she could give him.

Who did he think he was, anyway? All that guff

about 'just the evening, not the night'—and then at the
first opportunity he'd gone and made a pass at her! He
might claim he wasn't looking for just another one-
night stand, but how could it be anything else, on that
basis? And with the man who'd been so rude to her,
only that afternoon!

Of course she had been right to turn him down. She
couldn't have done anything else. Maybe her unas-
suaged body was protesting, but the hunger inside her
couldn't have been satisfied in a few short hours.

She turned the shower on full, pulled off her clothes,
and stood under the jet of lukewarm water for a long
time. Then she washed her hair, and rubbed it dry. The
monotonous actions acted like a slow valve, leaking
away the pressure of her longing. It wasn't so bad. She
hadn't really passed up on anything worth having.

And by now her body was beginning to agree, so
that soon after she had settled between the cool sheets
of the hotel bed she found sleep coming to claim her.

Brad was breakfasting in the hotel dining-room when
Tara came down the following morning. He was sitting
at the window-table where they had sat the night
before, but looking every inch the European manager
now, in a dark grey three-piece suit and a bright blue
shirt.

He waved her over when he saw her, and Tara
hesitated. She wasn't at all sure that his offer to let her
finish her inspection would have survived her rejection
of him. But it was soon apparent that it had, and that
he was determined to forget the incident in the town
centre, and behave to her in a friendly but businesslike
manner.

Annoyingly, she found it hard to copy his example.
It was easy to tell herself she had been right to say no

when he wasn't around; much harder, when he was gazing at her across the table with intent dark eyes. But, right or wrong, the moment for choice was gone now—after that day, she almost certainly wouldn't see him again.

Still, there was an awkwardness in the atmosphere as he asked her about her weekend plans, and she outlined the things she planned to do in Arles during the time that she might have spent with him.

After the waitress brought her coffee, he changed the subject to her insurance inspection. 'I've been thinking how it's best to handle things,' he said briskly. 'I did consider taking Morot straight back, and having him carry on as your guide, but there are too many problems. I don't mind overriding Fillol over the inspection, but the Morot situation needs proper investigation. I don't want you working alone, though—I meant it when I said you need protection. So I'll set Henri Sarlat to work with you this morning: he's Morot's deputy, and he seems a good kid.'

'But you will take up Jean-Claude's case?' Tara asked earnestly.

'Yeah—I promised to, and I will. But keep it cool, Tara. Don't say anything to Fillol, OK?'

'Of course not,' she assured him. 'And thank you, Brad—I do appreciate your helping me.'

Brad's help didn't stop there. Appreciating that she would find it difficult to confront Monsieur Fillol again, he accompanied her to the general manager's office once they had arrived back at the ECF factory, and told Fillol what arrangements he had made for her. The little manager sulked visibly, but he didn't have any choice but to comply. When Brad had left them he called in Henri Sarlat, a lanky matchstick of a boy with a red crew-cut, and told him to stay with Tara all the time she was on the premises.

'There's one more thing,' Tara said politely. 'At the very end of my inspection I need to discuss my recommendations with you. Could I make an appointment? Say, for this afternoon at four?'

'At four I'm busy,' Monsieur Fillol said huffily.

'I'll come later, then?'

'I can fit you in at five-thirty.'

Five-thirty! On Friday! She had hoped to be away from the factory well before then. But she followed Brad's advice to keep it cool, and meekly agreed that five-thirty would be fine.

It was a relief when Monsieur Fillol shooed her and Henri out of his office, and she was left to the security assistant's company. Pleasant company it was, too; Henri didn't have any of Jean-Claude's quick wit, but he was cheerful and willing to oblige her, and seemed genuinely interested in the tests she carried out on the fire pump and sprinkler system, hoses and hydrants.

They were in the pressing shop, checking the water pressure, when a murmured, 'Good afternoon, Tara,' in a twangy American accent had her jumping, and all but dropping her clipboard.

'Oh,' she said inadequately. 'Hello, Mr Hamilton.'

Brad half-raised a dark eyebrow, as if he was amused at her formality. 'How's it going?' he asked.

'It's looking OK. The sprinkler system's well designed, and the water pressure's good. I've got to do some final calculations, but I don't think there'll be any serious problems—except with the housekeeping, of course.'

'That don't mean much to me, I'm afraid.'

'It'll all be explained in my report.'

'So when do you finish?'

'I'll finish here by three, I guess, then I've got to wait till five-thirty to see Monsieur Fillol.'

'Five-thirty? Why?'

'That's the only time he could offer me.'

Brad looked very sceptical, but in front of Henri he could hardly make any comment. 'Take care, huh?' was all he said.

'I always do.'

'Yeah, I noticed. Not one for risks, are you?'

'Brad, just because I——'

''Scuse us, Sarlat,' Brad said smoothly. He took her arm and drew her towards the wall of the factory, out of earshot of Henri and the nearest operatives.

'Now look,' he said bluntly. 'I understand your attitude, but I don't agree with it. You're running away before you've found out what you're running from.'

'But Brad, it's impossible. We could never have more than a——'

'I don't like that word never,' he sharply interrupted her. 'I don't give up that easily, and nor do you, I'd have thought.'

'Not in the right cause, but——'

'So give it a chance. If you've got to be here till after five-thirty, you won't have time to get to Arles and find a hotel-room tonight. Stay on here another night, and have dinner with me again. We'll talk, OK? We can't talk here, but I need to talk to you. I don't want to see you slip through my fingers.'

Tara bit her lip, and, seeing her indecision, Brad moved a step closer, touching her hand with his. 'Please, Tara?'

It was that touch that melted her—the flame of hunger that leapt up in her, at the first brush of his fingers. Perhaps he was right, perhaps she was being too wary. Perhaps she was throwing up the chance of finding something rare and precious—and why?

She knew the answer—because she was afraid of being hurt. But did she really have to be hurt? If their relationship worked out well, mightn't they find a way to continue it? Wasn't it worth exploring the possibilities a little further? Didn't she owe herself that much?

He saw her uncertainty, and seized on it.

'Seven? No, we'll make it seven-thirty, if you'll be late back. I might as well grab the chance to stay on and do some extra work myself. I'll see you in the hotel bar at seven-thirty.'

He touched her hand again, just lightly, then turned and strode away. Tara's eyes followed him; then she refocused on Henri, standing awkwardly by a pressing-machine a few yards off; and next to him—though she hadn't seen him come in—the dapper little figure of Monsieur Fillol.

Monsieur Fillol couldn't have heard them, but he had obviously seen their exchange, and that thought brought a flush to her cheeks. From his snide expression, he was obviously coming to some very crude and inaccurate conclusions about Brad's change of heart towards her.

He didn't say anything, though, and she couldn't afford to take offence at a look. So she briskly nodded to him, collected together her equipment, and invited Henri to follow her to the site of her next test—the finished goods warehouse.

Henri was not a fast worker, and it was boring waiting for him to connect a hose to the riser—the pipe that fed the sprinkler system. Tara tapped her foot impatiently on the floor, glancing around the warehouse interior. It wasn't a pretty sight. The pallets of

finished-goods storage should have been neatly stacked
with gangways between them, but these were haphaz-
ardly jumbled, and in the far corner was a messy heap
of broken boxes. Then she pricked up her ears.

'Tara!'

That was what had caught her attention—a hissed
whisper, barely loud enough to be heard from where
she stood. She glanced uncertainly around her, not sure
where it had come from.

'Tara?'

'Over here,' she replied, in French.

A shadow appeared on the warehouse floor, then a
figure emerged from between the stacks of boxed
plastic kitchenware.

'Jean-Claude!'

'Sssh.' Jean-Claude Morot looked around furtively.
'You are alone?'

'No, Henri Sarlat's with me,' she whispered back.

'Oh, Henri's OK.' He relaxed. 'It's Fillol I need to
keep an eye open for.'

'What are you doing here, Jean-Claude? Have you
seen Mr Hamilton yet? Have you been reinstated?'

'Fat chance of that.' Jean-Claude scowled. 'I've
talked to my union representative, and he's told me
how to go about complaining of unfair dismissal.'

'Don't do that, Jean-Claude—not yet.'

'I haven't yet. I came back to see if you got any joy
out of Hamilton yesterday.'

'I think so,' Tara responded. 'He promised to investigate, and he wants to talk to you. Perhaps you could
go and find him now?'

'Talk! Huh!'

'No, seriously, Jean-Claude. He's sympathetic; he
just wants to investigate properly before he does anything. He's got to talk to you, and to Fillol too.'

'And you know who he'll believe, don't you?'

'You, I'd bet,' Tara said stoutly. 'He listened to me, and here I am finishing my inspection, with his and Fillol's agreement. He'll listen to you, too.'

Jean-Claude frowned. 'It's not much. I'm grateful to you, Tara, but saying he'll talk. . . It sounds to me as if he's just stalling.'

'You don't have to believe me,' Tara assured him. 'Talk to Mr Hamilton and see for yourself.'

'What do you think, Henri?' Jean-Claude asked.

Henri shrugged. 'I hope you stitch up Fillol, get him into really hot water.'

'The union man'll do that, he promised.'

'So will Br—Mr Hamilton,' Tara quickly amended. 'Jean-Claude, please. You owe it to me to try, after I went to plead with him.'

Jean-Claude considered. 'All right, I'll try. I'm not risking Fillol seeing me, though—I'll have to find a time when he's out of the way.'

'Fillol's seeing me at five-thirty, so he'll be tied up in his office then—and Mr Hamilton said he'd be working late tonight. That would be the ideal time to go to him, if you can wait that long. . .?'

'Thanks, Tara; I'll do that,' Jean-Claude agreed.

CHAPTER THREE

THE rest of Tara's inspection went smoothly, and by
two o'clock she was back in her hotel room, making
some last calculations and notes to prepare her for her
interview with Monsieur Fillol. She only had to give
him a short informal presentation of her findings; later,
Insco would send a printed report to a range of SHP's
top management.

It caused her a lot of thought, though, because ECF
Montelimar wasn't an easy location to summarise in
the way her underwriters expected.

Clients who were urged to pay out thousands of
pounds for fire pumps and sprinkler systems sometimes
didn't realise that the underwriters put even more stress
on housekeeping standards, and on an intangible factor
called 'management attitudes'. Experience had taught
them that well-run factories suffered far fewer fires
than poorly run ones, regardless of the level of protection equipment.

ECF under Monsieur Fillol certainly didn't rate as a
well-run factory—but arguably things were on the
brink of change. Under Brad and SHP the factory
would surely be tidied up, procedures tightened, fire-
drills practised. Could she give the company any credit
for that?

Reluctantly, she decided that she couldn't—and nor,
to be honest, did she want to. What she wanted was to
see Jean-Claude Morot reinstated and Monsieur Fillol
fired in his stead. Maybe her bad management ratings
would help to bring that about. Then, if Brad, and

whatever management he replaced Fillol with, did make improvements, that could be reflected in a dramatic rise in ratings when the next Insco inspector called in six months' time.

She did recall Brad's request that she tread carefully, but it didn't seem to her that she could let that sway her when she made her decisions. So she finally checked the 'poor' ratings on her report form, in the confidence that her boss Jim Backley would almost certainly agree with her judgement.

There was just time to freshen her face and comb through her hair before dashing back to the factory. She arrived at the gate at twenty past five, and had to wait several minutes to allow a stream of cars to leave the car park.

The pressing shop and warehouse worked only one shift, and for most of the workers this was knocking-off time. Many of the small-office staff were also leaving, and by the time Tara made her way along the corridor that led to Monsieur Fillol's office, the building was thick with after-hours silence.

It wasn't the best possible timing for what threatened to be an uncomfortable meeting, but she didn't let that worry her too much. Insurance inspectors rarely rated as top priority with any busy senior manager, so it wasn't unusual for her to have to hang around before she could carry out this final part of her assignment.

The light of Monsieur Fillol's office, glowing through the opaque glass fronting the corridor wall, struck a welcoming note as she knocked on the door to his office suite. 'Ah, Mademoiselle Miller,' Monsieur Fillol's secretary, Madeleine, greeted her. '*Monsieur* will be ready to see you in a few minutes.'

Tara sat, and chatted desultorily to the secretary as the latter tidied her office, and covered up her word processor. Madeleine reminded Monsieur Fillol that Tara was still waiting, then bade her goodbye, and set off home.

Fortunately, Tara didn't have to wait much longer before Monsieur Fillol, busily apologetic, ushered her into his office.

'It's been a long week, Mademoiselle Miller,' he said, as he moved back behind his desk. 'Let's celebrate the weekend to come. A glass of whisky?'

Tara was so taken aback by this apparent friendliness that it took her a moment to collect herself, and respond, 'Thank you, but I don't drink while I'm working.'

'You don't mind if I do?'

'Not at all,' she assured him. He took her at her word and went straight to a cupboard in the corner, pouring himself a generous half-tumbler of straight Scotch.

'This won't take long,' Tara said briskly, and as soon as he was seated she began to run through her recommendations.

Monsieur Fillol listened in silence, twirling the whisky tumbler around in his hands, and watching her with a greasy half-smile.

Though the verdict she was bringing wasn't a good one, she did her best to soften its impact, stressing how easy it would be to bring the factory up to standard, and praising everything there was to praise. Brad could have the hard work of leaning on Fillol to get things changed, backed up by Insco's underwriters, and their threat of increased rates.

'So that's it, basically,' Tara concluded. 'Another inspector will make a follow-up visit in six months, and if these recommendations are carried out you can hope for an excellent rating then.'

Monsieur Fillol eyed her greasily. 'Of course,' he said, quite suddenly, 'it's all that rat Morot's fault.'

'Pardon?'

'Morot. That ass of a security manager. It was his job keeping the fire precautions up to scratch. Now I've got rid of him, there should be no trouble putting everything right.'

Should there? Tara was too surprised to respond. That wasn't how she had analysed the situation at all. She had been certain that Fillol himself was the weak link.

Was she right, though? she wondered uneasily. She had taken readily to Jean-Claude Morot's impish charm, and had taken just as readily *against* Fillol's oily insinuations; she wanted to believe that Morot was the goodie, and Fillol the baddie. But likeability and good management skills weren't the same, were they?

'I certainly hope so,' she said, a little uncertainly.

'No doubt of it, my dear. Now let me persuade you to a whisky, and we'll drink to the end of your inspection.'

'Well, if you. . .'

Monsieur Fillol was already refilling his own glass, and pouring one for her. She couldn't really refuse the glass he pressed into her hand, or fail to take at least a sip from it.

'Yes, I've everything sorted out,' Fillol said confidently. 'There's a man I have in mind for the security manager job—my wife's brother, actually—so I can tell you, you've nothing to worry about.'

'I must say, I was—I *am*—worried about Monsieur Morot. I didn't feel he did anything wrong in helping me with the inspection, and——'

'Forget Morot,' Monsieur Fillol said sharply. 'That

man was trouble from the start. Don't let that regrettable incident cloud your stay in Montelimar. How do you like our lovely town?'

'It's charming, from the little I've seen.'

'You stay for the weekend?'

'No, only tonight.'

'But tonight you are here? So you must let me buy you dinner,'

'Thank you, but I. . . I'm busy tonight.'

'Ah.' Monsieur Fillol smiled knowingly. 'I think I guess who made you the offer first.'

Not difficult, Tara thought ruefully, especially when he'd witnessed her exchange with Brad that afternoon. It wasn't a comfortable realisation. Monsieur Fillol probably thought she had slept her way into Brad's favour, and she could hardly put him right.

She gave him a vague smile.

'Still, you have another drink with me, at least,' Monsieur Fillol urged.

'I've barely started this one.'

'You drink slow.' He, in contrast, was drinking fast. His second glassful had gone, and he rose to pour a third.

'It's a funny job you have, a pretty girl like you,' he went on, moving round the side of his desk towards Tara. 'So pretty—too pretty to work in factories. Your hair is the colour of sunshine. The colour of ripe wheat in the sun, and so soft. . .'

'Actually you get to be rather hard in my job,' Tara smartly retorted. 'Now if you'll excuse me, Monsieur Fillol, I really must be going.'

'You haven't finished your drink.'

'You've poured me more than I can manage when I'm driving, I'm afraid. You'll be sent a printed copy of my report, as I said, and. . .'

Almost frantically, she was stuffing papers back into her briefcase as she got to her feet. Fillol might be strong, but he was a small man, and though she wasn't afraid of him physically she certainly didn't want her inspection to end with the nasty scene that was threatening to develop if she didn't leave right away.

'And your eyes, such an unusual shade of blue. . . The blue of the Mediterranean at sunset. You must see our lovely sea, the Côte d'Azur. . .'

Monsieur Fillol's words were becoming slurred. Tara inched towards the door. Monsieur Fillol's arm shot out with unexpected speed and barred the way.

'Nice to have met you, Monsieur Fillol,' she said curtly.

'Nicer still to kiss you.'

'No, thank you.'

'Come on, come on. Just one little kiss.'

'Certainly not!' She was reaching out for the door-knob when her attention was diverted by a movement on the other side of the glass wall. Somebody was coming along the lighted corridor.

Monsieur Fillol, meanwhile, took rapid advantage of her lowered guard to grab her arms and pull her towards him.

'A lovely woman like you,' he murmured.

'No!' Tara staggered, and her foot slipped on the shiny floor, while her falling briefcase skidded right across the room. She was struggling to regain her balance and break free of Monsieur Fillol's determined grip when the door to the office was suddenly flung open.

'What the hell?' Brad Hamilton exclaimed.

Monsieur Fillol rapidly let go of Tara, and off-balance, she fell heavily to the tiled floor.

'Er. . . Mademoiselle Miller just slipped, and I was

trying to help her. . .' Monsieur Fillol reached out a hand to add believability to his excuse.

'You can't expect us to believe that!' Jean-Claude Morot held out a hand, too, as did Brad. Tara accepted Brad's, and let him pull her to her feet. He slipped his arm round her shoulders, holding her reassuringly close to him.

'You OK, Tara?' he asked, in a low voice.

'I'll live.'

'What happened?'

'You saw,' she said ruefully, rubbing the sore spot where she'd landed.

'I can guess, but I didn't see clearly through the glass. Can you bear to tell me?'

'He made a pass, didn't he?' Jean-Claude demanded.

Tara nodded. 'At least, he grabbed me. You came so quickly, he didn't——'

'But he would have raped you if we hadn't come,' Jean-Claude insisted.

Would he? Tara hadn't really felt afraid before Brad came in, and now she was no more than slightly shaken from her fall. She felt perfectly capable of weighing up the situation objectively—and she guessed that Fillol wouldn't have raped her, or even come close to it. Harassment was nasty enough, and he was certainly guilty of that, but she doubted he'd been drunk or crazy enough to push her any further. And even if he had, she felt confident that she would have been able to fight him off.

But she could also see that Jean-Claude wanted—and needed—to milk the situation for all it was worth. The last thing he wanted was for her to defend Fillol, now that the manager had been caught in a compromising situation.

Looking on the gloomy side, it wasn't hard for her to

give a convincing tremble. 'It was horrible,' she said unsteadily. 'He started drinking, and——'

'Just a minute,' Brad interrupted. 'Drinking what?'

'Whisky—from that cupboard over there.'

'Fillol, is this true?'

'I only keep it for visitors,' Fillol said cringingly. 'Mademoiselle Miller asked for a drink, and——'

'I did not!'

'That's enough. Then what happened, Tara?'

'Then he started paying me silly compliments, and I said I'd got to go, but he blocked my way, and asked for a kiss, and grabbed me. And then you burst in.'

'Thank goodness,' Brad said forbiddingly. 'Fillol, you'll apologise to Miss Miller.'

'It was her fault,' the manager said peevishly. 'A woman on her own—she asks for it. And gets it—that's easy enough to see.'

'And what's that supposed to mean?' Brad demanded, his hand tightening on Tara's shoulder.

Fillol seemed to realise, belatedly, that he'd made an extremely bad move. His eyes shifted from side to side. 'Well. . .' he said uneasily. Then, triumphantly, 'Morot! Ever since she arrived, she was all over him. She wasn't turning *him* down when——'

'That's *enough*!' Brad's body was rigid, his grip painful on her shoulder, his lips narrowed into a thin line. 'Tara,' he said, loosening his hold, but not turning to her, 'wait outside for me, please.'

She didn't need a second invitation. Halfway down the corridor to the outside door, she heard footsteps, and spun round warily—but it was only a jubilant Jean-Claude, who had obviously been given his marching orders too.

'Tara, that was fantastic.'

'That's hardly the word I'd use for it,' she said

viciously. Maybe it would get Jean-Claude his job back, but she felt sickened and cheapened by the whole incident.

'No—I mean, it was awful, but you were wonderful. So brave!'

'Thanks for nothing!' His face fell, and she added, more gently, 'Sorry, Jean-Claude. Maybe it made all the difference for you, but I'm just sick of this place, and I can't wait to get away.' She pushed open the outer door, and headed towards the car park.

'Monsieur Hamilton said to wait. . .' Jean-Claude called after her.

'Monsieur Hamilton can go hang himself.'

It was not quite seven o'clock when Tara got back to her hotel. Arles wasn't so far; she could surely get there and find somewhere to stay before it was too late for supper. She tossed her suitcase on to the bed and began to throw into it the few outfits she had hung in the wardrobe.

She hadn't quite finished her packing when there was a knock on her door. She ignored it. She didn't want to talk to him now.

Brad—and it could only have been Brad—clearly hadn't any intention of being ignored, though. His gentle raps, and calls of 'Tara, are you there?' rapidly escalated into a loud hammering accompanied by shouts of 'I know you're in there, dammit! Let me in!'

'Go away!' she shouted, in French.

'No way am I going away!'

'*Monsieur, s'il vous plaît*!' a refined French voice interrupted. '*Je veux du repos*!'

'*Pardon, Madame. Mais*. . . Tara! Please!'

'Damn you, Brad Hamilton!' Tara muttered under

her breath, reluctantly opening her door, and immediately retreating to the far side of the room.

'That took you long enough,' Brad remarked.

'Maybe I thought you'd get the message!'

'What message?'

'That I don't want to see you!'

'Don't be ridiculous!'

'So what's ridiculous about that?'

'All right,' Brad growled, moving towards her, then thinking better of it and prowling to the window instead, 'you're upset. But I'm not Fillol.'

'I'd never have noticed!'

'Tara!'

'Now look at it from my angle,' Tara retorted heatedly. 'It's all right you blaming Fillol, and OK, he's a skunk, and he deserves all he gets. But I bet he'd never have pushed his luck that far if he hadn't seen *you* getting away with it earlier.'

'And what's that supposed to mean?'

'In the pressing shop. He saw you making up to me there—and do you know what he thought? And what Henri thought, and most likely everyone else in that factory? They all saw you throw me out yesterday, and they all saw me come back in with you this morning, and don't tell me you can't guess what was going through their minds!'

'Oh, for heaven's sake!'

'All right, they were wrong, but they weren't that far wrong, were they? So Fillol thought a woman on her own in a factory was fair game—and what did *you* think? *You* thought it was worth pushing me to jump into bed with you! *You* thought you could grab me and kiss me in your office! It's all right you throwing the book at Fillol, but just you take a look at the mote in your own eye!'

'That wasn't the same at all!' Brad retorted.

'Oh, wasn't it? What's the difference, then? You think you're better-looking than him—is that it? So it's all right for a man to harass a woman if he's good-looking, because then he can kid himself she likes it!'

'Dammit, you did like it!'

'And how were you to know that when you grabbed at me?'

Brad glared at her for a long, tense moment; then he subsided, shoulders drooping, to sit on the edge of her bed.

'What you've got to understand, Tara,' he said more measuredly, 'is that you're in a dangerous position. Maybe you don't mean to provoke men, but you do, just because you're a woman—a beautiful woman—and on your own. All right, I shouldn't have touched you, and I've already apologised for that. But can't you see? As long as you keep on doing that job you're going to suffer from men trying it on. That's what gets me. You can twist it all you like, but what gets to me is the thought of what might have happened this evening, if Morot and I hadn't come along when we did.'

Tara glared for a moment more, then she moved over to stand in front of him.

'You know what would have happened?' she asked, in a level voice.

'You surely don't need it spelling out.'

'No, but you do, Brad Hamilton, because the picture in your mind's the wrong picture.' She paused, then said, more quietly still, 'Let me tell you. OK, Fillol's a pain. I know his kind, and there are all too many of them around. They'll push their luck in all directions, sex included. But they're no fools, and they don't reckon to end up in gaol for rape. Fillol didn't do more than try to grab a kiss, and I told you, I don't believe he'd have tried even that if he hadn't seen me with you, and misread what he saw.'

'But men *do* misjudge women in your situation.'

'Sometimes, true—but in more ways than one. I may look fragile, but I know how to look after myself. If he had tried anything more, I know quite a few moves that would have stopped him in his tracks. And although it was late, I knew you were still in the office block, and Jean-Claude was there too, so help would have come if I'd called out.'

'This time, maybe. But is that always so?'

'Situations always differ—but Brad, it's no good your overestimating the danger. There's danger everywhere, but people don't let that stop them living life to the full. I've been doing my job for three years now, and although all too many men have made comments I could do without, very few have so much as touched me, and none of them have got me really frightened.'

'Maybe I over-reacted,' Brad said slowly.

'A little.' She smiled, awkwardly. 'What did you do, after I left?'

'Gave him a formal warning. I didn't fire him, but it's a step towards doing that if he doesn't shape up pretty soon. And I ordered him to reinstate Morot.'

'That's good news.'

'I thought you'd maybe be disappointed that I didn't fire him straight off.'

Tara shrugged. 'He's a bad manager. You'd be better off without him.'

'Maybe so, but I'm not doing anything until I've thought it through. I've only been at the plant three days, after all—and I don't yet know who I'd put in Fillol's place if I did fire him.'

She nodded. That made sense. It surprised her a little that he'd exercised that much restraint. She had seen him as an aggressive manager—one who would rarely under-react to a situation. But maybe, she thought, the way he'd behaved over her wasn't so typical of him after all.

'Still,' Brad went on, 'it's been a long week, and I'm glad to see the end of it.' He got to his feet, and she tensed, expecting him to touch her; but he didn't, instead striding back again to the window. He stood there, silhouetted against a reddening sky. She could see the tenseness in his loose-limbed body, in the set of his shoulders, the stance of his feet.

'You must be sick of this place,' he said slowly, 'and I can't blame you one bit. And maybe I don't know when to give up, but I don't want you hating me, too. I don't want you to be alone tonight, either. So will you still come to eat with me? Please?'

'Brad, you're asking for more than I want to give.' And yet she didn't want him to leave, either, she thought silently. She might have resented his rescuing her from Fillol, but oh, she had been glad to see him, and glad of the protection he had given her.

'I'm only asking for supper. Supper, and a chance to talk to you.'

'Are you?' She shook her head, though he was still looking away from her, and wouldn't see the gesture. 'Brad—maybe it's unfair, because what happened earlier wasn't your fault, but I'd rather you left me alone tonight.'

'We've only got tonight.'

'We haven't really got that,' she responded drily. And he didn't push her further, but strode to the door, and slammed it behind him in a way that must have had her complaining neighbour wincing.

CHAPTER FOUR

TARA woke on Saturday morning in a bright rush, like the sun streaming through the window of her hotel room. She knew there was something to make her happy. But, like a dream barely remembered, she couldn't quite set her finger on what it was—and then came the ghastly realisation. She had been dreaming of Brad, and now she was waking to the cold knowledge that she had turned down all his overtures, and was left to spend the weekend alone.

Which wasn't so bad, was it? She spent lots of weekends alone, when she was working far away from home. She enjoyed her own company, and she knew how to entertain herself. What was more, she was going to Arles, reputedly a lovely town, with a mass of things to see: Roman ruins, medieval churches, and the glorious scenery of Provence.

It should have been enough to raise her spirits, but it wasn't. Still, she did her best, splashing on perfume, picking some of her most relaxed and cheerful clothes—tight off-white jeans and a slash-necked pink sweatshirt—and lingering over the light breakfast that she ate in her room, for fear Brad might be in the hotel dining-room.

He might, come to that, have been in the lobby when she paid her bill, or on the street as she loaded her bags into her car. But he wasn't. There wasn't any reason for her to be annoyed about that—quite the opposite, in fact—so she put her irritability down to tiredness, turned up the car radio, and set off down the Autoroute du Soleil.

It was another fine day, with the sun blazing from a clear blue sky, and only the faintest hint of breeze in the air. The journey to Arles was fast and enjoyable— first down the motorway that followed the Rhône valley as far as Avignon, then along a long, straight road that cut through typically Provençal scenery, where the vineyards of the river valley gave way to flat maize and sunflower fields edged with ditches. Then came the city itself, rising out of the flat landscape, the stone gates, and the narrow winding streets of the old town.

She had already booked into a small hotel just by the huge Roman amphitheatre, and to her delight it was not only easy to find, but looked perfectly charming. At the front, café tables interspersed with tubs of flowers spilled across the pavement. There was no car park, but she was able to find a temporary parking space down a side-road while she unloaded her case.

Parked in the next space was a red Ferrari.

What an odd coincidence! Or. . . No, it couldn't be. Arles was about eighty miles from Montelimar—there wasn't any possibility of Brad's being there. Red Ferraris weren't so very uncommon, and this was obviously someone else's red Ferrari. All the same, she moved closer to the car and glanced inside, but its empty interior told her nothing, and she didn't recall the number of Brad's car.

It couldn't really be his. Men like Brad didn't persist when they had been rejected. She turned her back on the car, and busied herself checking in to the hotel. Her room was just as pleasant as the look of the outside had promised: cool and shady, with heavy old wooden furniture, including a big old-fashioned bed.

She settled herself in, bought a guidebook, and read

it while drinking coffee at one of the café tables, then wandered over the road and paid the entrance fee to the amphitheatre.

It was a vast building, built of a daunting grey stone. A chilling passageway led from the entrance through to the arena—a huge empty circular space. Bathed in sunlight, it was surrounded by the tiers of stone seating that had been constructed by the Romans, some of them overlaid by modern wooden bench-seats.

Tara clambered part-way up the steep steps, made her way along a narrow aisle, then sat down on a bench, drinking in the sunshine and the splendour of the view.

The arena wasn't crowded. A sprinkling of tourists were exploring it, but in the enormous space they made little impression. There were a young couple, scrambling hand in hand over the top of the topmost row of arches; some voluble French children, running up and down the stairs; over on the other side of the arena, half a dozen others.

A tall man, dark-haired, with a large, loose-limbed body, dressed in grey trousers and a yellow cotton jumper, was standing near the base of the tiers of seats, and gazing across the empty arena at her.

No. It couldn't be. From a distance it might look like him, but it couldn't be.

He couldn't really be looking at her. But she didn't like the feeling that he was, and uneasily she got up and made her way to the nearest exit.

Behind the arena was a maze of passages and stone steps, some of them leading to an outer arcade, flanked by a row of tall arches. Tara wandered around here, savouring the contrast between the chilly shadows and the half-moons of warmth where the sun struck its way through the arches. She found the crumbling grandeur of the amphitheatre rather forbidding, but it was certainly impressive.

This part of the monument was even more deserted than the arena, and as she moved further away from the entrance she found herself quite alone. Then the curve of the walkway suddenly revealed to her the figure of a man, approaching from the opposite direction, and already a bare ten yards from her.

Brad. Unmistakable, now. Instinctively, she stopped in her tracks, her eyes searching for one of the side passages—but she was some distance from the nearest one, and before she could move towards it he was at her side.

'I wondered how long it would take you,' he said conversationally.

'How long! You mean——'

'You told me you were going to start your sightseeing here—which was obvious, anyway. Staying at a hotel right opposite, you'd hardly walk past it, would you?'

'And how would you know where I'm staying?'

'I worked through the Michelin Guide, phoning every hotel till I hit the right one. You chose very well, incidentally.'

'Thanks,' Tara said automatically; then she registered the meaning of what he'd said. 'You're not staying there too?'

'I thought it'd be more convenient if we were in the same place.' Brad smiled. 'Come on, Tara. We're not in Montelimar now. You can forget all about Fillol and the rest, but I wasn't having you forget about me.'

'But. . .' Her voice faded away. She had been meaning to protest, but suddenly that seemed to her not merely pointless, but stupid. Really, she was immensely glad to see him. The weekend had moved from shade to sunlight with the realisation that he'd come all this way to see her. Maybe there were dangers in getting to know him better, but much more immediate was the pleasure she was already feeling.

Brad wisely didn't push his point, but accepted her mute acquiescence. 'Have you seen everything here?' he enquired. 'Then let's go. I'll buy you an ice-cream, and we'll move on to St Trophime.'

'It'll serve you right if you hate churches and Roman ruins,' she warned him. 'Because I plan to look at them all.'

'Actually, I enjoy them,' he assured her, taking her arm as they crossed the road to the nearest café. 'I'd been meaning to come here some time while I was based in Montelimar. But my passion's Van Gogh, so this afternoon's going to be devoted to him.'

'Don't I get a say?'

Brad paused to order and pay for two large chocolate cornets. Then, 'In what I do today? Not much,' he said calmly. 'This morning I'll be following you, and this afternoon I pay homage to my master, as I just told you. You can follow me, or you can go your own way, if you prefer.'

'And this evening?'

He smiled again, his eyes holding hers. 'You can eat on your own, if you like.'

'Does anyone like eating on their own?'

'Not in my experience. Not me, anyway—that's why I'm inviting you to have dinner with me.'

'Thank you, sir.'

'My pleasure,' he said sardonically. 'Now hold my cornet for a moment, and I'll just look at the map and see which street we have to take.'

Tara had been determined to enjoy herself alone, but enjoying herself with Brad turned out to be a lot easier.

He was a relaxed but enthusiastic tourist, determined to see everything, but happy to linger wherever she chose. The twelfth-century church of St Trophime, with its carved west front and its beautiful shady cloisters, delighted them both.

Then they found a café at which to eat a light lunch of pizza and salad—and again they lingered, drinking wine and enjoying the sunshine.

Brad talked about Van Gogh. It was clearly a subject he knew backwards. He'd talked intelligently about church architecture, so Tara wasn't surprised by his being well-informed, but still the depth of his knowledge about the painter astonished her. He outlined Van Gogh's career, then told her in detail about the period he had spent in Arles, and the pictures he had painted there, including the classic *Sunflowers*. It was there, too, that he had cut off his ear, and spent a period in a psychiatric institution.

Tara had known these famous details, but the rest of the story was largely unfamiliar to her. She had imagined that the painter was a raving madman. Not so, Brad insisted. It had taken discipline as well as genius to produce some of the greatest paintings of all time. Only at a few moments of great stress had Van Gogh's mental control completely failed him.

'He's a real obsession with you, isn't he?' she commented, when he paused to draw breath.

'Obsession? No,' Brad thoughtfully replied. 'That implies an unblanaced interest, and I don't think mine is unbalanced. Van Gogh has been a major influence on most twentieth-century painters. Scratch almost any one of them, and I should think they could tell you as much about him as I could.'

'But you're not a twentieth-century painter.'

He shrugged. 'In a small way I am.'

'That's your hobby? Really?'

Somewhere, she'd struck a wrong note. She could see it in his face, but she had no idea what her gaffe had been. The enthusiasm with which he had been talking had vanished, though, and it was in a distant manner that he replied, 'I don't do much now.'

'But you used to?'

'Yes.' He stood up abruptly, scraping his metal chair against the pavement, and announcing, 'We ought to get going. I'll just pay the bill.'

Tara didn't follow him; she sat, watching him carve an awkward route between the tightly crammed tables.

Brad, a painter? It wasn't the hobby she would have expected of a forceful businessman—and it would have been difficult to imagine anything more at odds with her first impression of him. But she had sensed all along that this businessman wasn't quite like any of the others she had known, and she had a suspicion that that half-regretted admission might prove to be the key to explaining why.

She would have liked to know more, but it would have threatened their happy mood if she had pushed him on the subject when he was so obviously reluctant to talk. So she held back her curiosity, and returned to the topic of Van Gogh as they left the café.

'So what is there to look at? According to my guidebook, none of Van Gogh's great paintings are here.'

'True,' Brad admitted. 'There's no Van Gogh museum, nothing spectacular to remember him by. But this is a town he lived and worked in, and many features of it have barely changed since his day. We can look at the sights he looked at, and painted, and immortalised. He painted the house where he lived with Gauguin, for instance—a yellow ochre house on a street corner. OK, it's a very ordinary house, not much different from a million others, but it's also a special house, because Van Gogh's vision of that house affected the way in which we see all houses today. So I want to look at it.'

And so they did. Taking pity on Tara's comparative ignorance, Brad also tracked down—with difficulty—a postcard reproduction of the Van Gogh painting, so that she could compare the raw material with the artist's vision.

Arles was a pleasant town, but still, its dusty streets in the afternoon heat were commonplace enough; its shops and houses no different from those of a thousand other small French towns. It was the artist's genius which had turned them into things of wonder. It was a tribute to Brad's own skill that he managed to convey some of that wonder to Tara.

It was a new idea to her, that what an artist had painted over a hundred years earlier could affect the way in which she herself saw the world. Brad insisted that it was so—that every person's vision was given structure and meaning by our artistic heritage. Fascinated, Tara began to understand what he meant, and how the Provence she saw now was a Provence of colours and shapes that had been indelibly stamped into her subconscious long before she had visited the area for herself.

Brad was not only a good teacher, though: he had, she felt sure, a fine artist's eye himself. In every view— and not only the few immortalised by Van Gogh and his contemporaries—he saw both interesting small details, and larger harmonies of colour and form.

'Doesn't it make you ache to paint these views yourself?' she asked, amused as well as impressed by his enthusiasm for so much that wasn't at all what she would have described as 'pretty'.

'Yes—and no. I'm not explaining it to you as a painter; I'm explaining it as a lover of Van Gogh. Do you understand? It's his vision that I'm trying to put across to you, not mine. And really, I don't have a personal vision of these sights. It's too much his territory—or perhaps what I mean is that I'm not a good enough artist to absorb his vision, and then move on to develop my own.'

'It sounds very complicated.'

'Serious art *is* complicated. In its way, I think it's the most intellectually demanding of all disciplines.'

'Harder than running a large company?'

'Hard in a different way.'

'No wonder you don't paint much any more. You don't make it sound like the ideal way of relaxing after a hard week at work.'

'*Relaxing*?' He threw her a look almost of contempt. 'Oh, no. Painting well isn't at all relaxing. Fulfilling, yes, but not relaxing.'

'So is that why you don't do it any more?'

'That's one reason,' Brad said slowly. 'I can't spare the mental effort at the moment—it all has to go into my work. It's a simplification—what motive isn't?— but it's not far off the truth.'

'When did you stop?'

'Six years ago.'

He answered readily, surprising her; after all, he'd usually clammed up whenever she'd risked a personal question. Had he forgotten to be wary, or had he deliberately decided to be more open? She glanced at him, but he wasn't looking back at her, and his face didn't tell her the answer.

What was more, his reply in itself had surprised her. He'd been so precise, as if he hadn't gradually let his painting tail away, but had quite suddenly decided not to do it any more.

'Why then? I mean, did something change in your life then? Something else?'

'Everything changed.'

Everything? What? How? This time she knew without asking that he wasn't going to tell her, though. He hurried them on from the corner where they'd stopped—almost, Tara thought, as if the ghost of Van Gogh was running after him, calling to him to keep painting, and he wanted to outdistance it.

Tara up-ended her suitcase on her big, high bed. She pulled a midnight-blue, scoop-necked top out of the pile of clothes, and held it against her, frowning critically into the mirror on her wardrobe door.

The softly clinging fabric and low neck made it sexier than most of her clothes—not that that was saying much, she thought ruefully. She didn't generally pack alluring outfits when she was travelling. Why should she? Usually the message she tried to give men was a definite 'no, thanks'.

That wasn't the message she wanted to put across tonight. So was she trying to give Brad a 'yes, please'? No, she wouldn't have gone that far. She just wanted to leave her options open. He'd claimed he wanted to talk to her about their situation, and he hadn't yet done so. Tonight he would talk. And she would listen, and then make up her mind whether becoming more involved with him was the right thing to do.

No bra—her small, high breasts didn't really need one, anyway. A softly flared skirt to match the top; a couple of thin gold chains to go round her neck, and two thicker gold bangles for her arm; high-heeled navy pumps. Leaving these laid out on the bed, she ducked under the shower, washed her hair and rubbed it dry.

No pony-tail. Pony-tails were for work, and this definitely wasn't work. She tried the effect of leaving her hair hanging loose, decided it wasn't quite right, and scooped up the sides in two enamelled slides.

Make-up: blue and violet eyeshadows, and mascara to make her eyes seem larger. Blusher and deep-coral lipstick. Perfume: St Laurent's *Opium*, musky and erotic.

Her mind strayed to Brad, getting ready in another single room, somewhere in the same small hotel. Brad in the shower, his big strong body glistening with water droplets. Brad smiling. Brad also away from work, relaxing, dressing for a special date.

He'd be dressed now. She had promised to meet him in the bar at seven-thirty, and it was twenty-five to eight already. Well, why not be late? Tara the business-woman was always on time, but this different Tara could surely afford a little feminine unpredictability.

She gave her reflection a last quick once-over, then picked up her bag and made her way downstairs.

Brad was standing at the counter, waiting for her. He'd changed too, she noted approvingly, matching his grey trousers with a cream silk shirt and soft grey leather blouson.

She watched his eyes widen as he took in her appearance.

'What you ordered, sir?'

'Exactly what I ordered,' he said, with a slow smile. 'I knew all along that there was a beautiful woman hiding behind that virago I met at the factory.'

'Not hiding,' Tara sharply retorted. 'The virago's me too—it's just a different side of me. Are we eating here?'

'No, we're going somewhere special.'

He took her to a small restaurant hidden away in the heart of the old town. From the outside it looked unremarkable, but inside it was charming in a slightly faded way, and the menu was enough to make her drool.

'I love France,' Tara said with a sigh of contentment, once they'd ordered their meal and were sitting sipping Pernods. 'Some of my colleagues feel it's a difficult place for an English person to work, but I always feel at home here.'

'Maybe that's because you speak the language so well,' Brad offered.

'That's a part of it, but only a part. I've been coming here since I was a child, but there's always something new to discover.'

'There's plenty to see in Arles,' Brad agreed. 'It's one of the most beautiful places in a beautiful country.'

'Did you choose to come here? Or did SHP send you?'

'Both.'

'That's not much of an answer,' she said critically.

'Sorry.' He shifted in the narrow restaurant chair, which clearly hadn't been made for a man of his dimensions, and stared into his wine glass. 'I'm not used to talking about myself.'

'But that's why you came, isn't it? To talk to me? Or did you just come so you could have another try at getting me into bed?'

'Both.' He recognised the echo of his previous answer, and smiled wryly. 'I wanted to see you again. I wanted—I still want—to know you better, in every way. And OK, that means having you know me better, too—but it's a long time since I opened up to another person, Tara.'

'Six years?'

'Six. . .? Oh. No, longer than that. Since I was married, really.'

'Did she leave you?'

He shrugged. 'It wasn't as tidy as that. Really, Adrienne was the sort of person you couldn't own. She married me, but somehow she never committed herself to me. She was always a free spirit, always off doing her own thing. We had rows all the time, and our marriage gradually fell apart. When she left it was to live with someone else, but it wasn't him that finished us, so much as the fact that we wanted different things out of our relationship.'

'But it hurt you.'

'Oh, yeah, it hurt.' He closed his eyes for a moment, as if he was recalling the pain of it. 'I wanted to give her so much, but she just didn't want it from me. And I always wanted things from her that she couldn't give.'

'What kind of things?' Tara asked softly.

'Closeness. Support. Belief in me, in what I was doing.'

'That wasn't so difficult, surely.'

'Sure it was. Adrienne was like a mirror; she only believed in people who believed in themselves. If I told her my work was great, she'd agree; if I told her I wasn't too sure about it, she'd tell me it was lousy. And that wasn't what I wanted to hear.'

'But you must have been successful, surely.' Tara frowned; she couldn't square the picture Brad was drawing with her own picture of him as a high-flying businessman. 'To get where you are now, you must have been doing well in those days.'

'Hell, if I'd been doing well then, I wouldn't be here now,' Brad said grittily.

'I don't understand.'

'No, you don't, do you?' He leaned forward, suddenly intent on explaining. 'I wasn't the same man then as you see now. You see Brad Hamilton the businessman, just as I saw Tara Miller the insurance inspector when I first met you. And boy, was she tough! But scratch her, and there's someone quite different inside that hard shell: a soft, vulnerable woman. Well, scratch me and you'll find a failed painter.'

'A failed painter!' Tara echoed, incredulously.

He laughed, but there was a bitter edge to his laughter. 'You want to know what happened six years ago? That's what happened. I stopped being a painter, and turned into a plastics executive.'

'Brad, I don't understand. You mean you were a proper painter? A full-time painter?'

'Yeah—for seven years, from age nineteen to twenty-six.'

'Tell me about it.'

He shrugged. 'It's not that interesting. I studied art in the States for a couple of years, then I came across to Paris and tried painting there. I did landscapes mainly, in oils. It was a great life in its way; Paris was a great place to live. I married Adrienne—she was an actress, just starting out—and we lived in an apartment high up in a big block on the Left Bank. But I was no Van Gogh, no tortured genius. I was just a spoilt rich-kid who wanted to be a famous artist.'

'Brad, you're being too hard on yourself.'

He shook his head, vehemently. 'If I am, it's only because I was too soft on myself back then. I can even feel sorry for Adrienne now, married to a whinging boy who wanted to be told he was marvellous all the time. But I wasn't marvellous, and deep down I knew it.'

'So you gave it up?'

'In the end—long after I should have done. I

should have thrown in the towel after Adrienne left, but I wanted to prove her wrong. I wanted to make it big so I could spit in her eye. How inane it sounds now!'

'I think it's understandable,' Tara said gently.

'Then my grandfather died,' Brad went on, his voice hardening, 'and I had to go back to the States. To join the family firm. I hated it then, but, looking back it was the best thing that ever happened to me. I'm a damn sight better manager than I ever was a painter.'

'I can believe that,' Tara agreed. 'But if that's so, why did you leave the family firm?'

Brad opened his mouth to reply; then a second thought seemed to catch him, and he hesitated.

'I'll tell you that another time,' he said offhandedly.

'But Brad, there won't be another time. On Monday I move on. We'll most likely never see each other again.'

'That doesn't have to be so,' Brad said levelly. 'You're giving up too quickly. I told you I wanted to get to know you better, and I do—but that's not just so we can have a great weekend, then grit our teeth and say goodbye. If it works out, if we find it's going to be hard to say goodbye, then we won't say it. We'll find a way to meet up again. If we want to enough, I reckon we can make something more of this.'

A tremble began in Tara's knees, and began to creep upwards. She clasped her hands together, tightly, to try to quell it.

'Brad,' she said unsteadily, 'I wish you were right, but I can't see it. You don't understand what my job's like. I'm travelling almost all the time, not only in France, but across Europe, and sometimes even further afield. I get assignments at short notice, most of the time. There's no way we could carry on a relationship like that. I've seen a couple of my colleagues try, and I can tell you, it doesn't work.'

'Then something would have to give—like your job.'

'You're serious?'

'Absolutely.' His dark eyes, holding hers across the restaurant table, confirmed his words. 'Tara,' he said earnestly, 'I'm not making promises now. It's too soon for that. I've made mistakes before, and one thing they've taught me is not to act too fast. I just want you to tell me that if your job and our relationship don't fit together, then you won't automatically choose your job over me.'

His hands enfolded her clasped ones—big, warm, comforting. His eyes seemed to look right into her, Tara stared back, mesmerised.

'I. . . This has never happened to me before,' she said unsteadily. 'I've never known a man I'd even think of throwing up my job for.'

'Never?' he asked, almost amused.

'No. Oh, I've had boyfriends. I had one when I started this job. He was a nice guy, the nicest boyfriend I'd ever had. I thought I loved him. When the job made it hard for me to see him as often as we wanted, he pushed me to give it up.'

'But you didn't?'

She shook her head. 'Brad, I wasn't even tempted. I asked him to let things ride for a while—six months, maybe—but he gave me an ultimatum. Marry him and change my job straight away, or he'd stop seeing me altogether. So I called his bluff, and it wasn't bluff. He went, and three months later he married my best friend.'

'That must have been pretty rough.'

She smiled, sadly. 'Strangely, it wasn't. Angie suited him so well. I was a little miffed that he married her so fast, but I can't pretend I was heartbroken. I had a think about it, and it seemed to me that I just wasn't the passionate type. If I didn't really want to marry a nice man like John, I wasn't likely ever to want to marry anyone. I didn't even miss him, particularly.'

'And there's been no one since?'

'No.'

'That must make for a lonely life.'

'It doesn't usually seem so.' She stared at her hands, clasped in his, so much bigger. 'Last night it seemed lonely,' she said slowly. 'Last night, and the night before.'

'It did for me, too,' Brad said softly. 'That's why I'm here, Tara.'

'I see,' she whispered.

'Still,' Brad continued, more briskly, 'that's enough raking over old embers for one night. Now where shall we go tomorrow?'

They discussed the options, lightly but in a friendly manner, over the remains of their delicious supper. Brad was all for hiring horses and exploring the Camargue, the region of lake and marshland to the south of Arles, while Tara fancied a more restful day.

Finally they compromised, agreeing to drive down in the Ferrari to Les Saintes-Maries-de-la-Mer, a small resort just by the mouth of the Little Rhône. The journey there would show them something of the scenery Brad was so eager to see, and the beaches would give Tara an opportunity to laze and sunbathe while he fitted in a swim.

Brad wasn't the kind of man who would ever be happy whiling away his holidays with nothing more than a paperback and a glass of wine, Tara thought to herself; he had an active, restless nature. There had been something less positive than restlessness about the man she had first met in the factory yard at Montelimar, though. There, she'd sensed in him a kind of nervous tension that surely wasn't good for him.

It was still strange to think of him as a laid-back painter, living among the café society in Paris. She could understand why he didn't want to go back to that way of life, but it seemed to her that he had perhaps put it too firmly behind him. He needed to come to terms with that creative side of his personality, not to suppress it—just as they both needed to come to terms with their emotional needs.

She felt very close to him as they walked back through the dark streets to their little hotel, his arm wrapped round her shoulders, his shadow looming huge in the glow from the streetlamps. This, she thought, would be one night in which neither of them was lonely. But Brad didn't come to her room, instead saying goodnight to her in the hotel corridor.

'Better not to rush things,' he said softly. 'No need. Somehow, we'll make the time to get to know each other properly.'

Yes—they would—but she was impatient. It wasn't enough for him to run his hand through the heavy loose mass of her hair, to draw her body up to meet his, to give her a kiss of piercing sweetness. She wanted the rest, too.

'I want you to stay tonight,' she whispered.

There was a smile playing around Brad's lips as he silently shook his head. 'No, Tara. I want you to be surer than this. I want you to want me more.'

'I want you enough already.'

He kissed her again, this time with tantalising light-ness, his lips just touching the corners of her mouth, the tip of her nose, the curve of her temple beneath the fall of her hair. 'Tomorrow,' he murmured, 'you'll want me much, much more.'

CHAPTER FIVE

'GREAT weather,' Brad said in a satisfied voice, as he tossed the bag containing his and Tara's possessions— towels, a couple of paperbacks, cans of soft drink— down on to the pebbly beach at Les Saintes-Maries-de-la-Mer. 'Swimming weather.'

'I doubt it,' Tara rejoined. 'It's barely June, remember. I know the sun's shining, but I bet that water's icy still.'

'You're talking to a guy who grew up on the Atlantic seaboard! In Massachusetts we don't expect hot baths when we take a dip—and after years of that, the Med in June's gonna suit me fine, I can tell you.'

'You can swim alone, then.'

'You're chicken,' he teased. And he threw off his jeans and bright green polo-shirt as if he meant to make straight for the water—but he didn't, stopping instead to spread his beach towel over the pebbles, and to fish in the bag for a bottle of suntan oil.

He barely needed it, Tara thought appreciatively, as her eyes roamed down an expanse of finely muscled bare chest, then skimmed more rapidly over brief black trunks, only to linger on his heavily corded thighs. His skin was the type to tan effortlessly, and she guessed he had already spent a few spare Sundays stretched out in the sunshine.

Fully dressed, Brad Hamilton was well worth a second glance, but, all-but-undressed, the sight of him took her breath away, and her voice was dangerously unsteady as she offered to rub the oil in for him.

'Sure,' he agreed, obligingly stretching out on the towel, and presenting a long expanse of back to her.

'Let me just take my skirt off, then I won't get it greasy.'

Feeling so aware of him, so oddly self-conscious, she was rather glad that he was lying down and couldn't admire her quite as blatantly as she was admiring him, as she stripped down to a skimpy denim-look bikini.

She knelt on the pebbles next to him, unscrewed the bottle, and reached out a cautious hand to his shoulder-blades. His skin was smooth and elastic, yielding slightly to her touch, as she dribbled the oil on to her palm and then began to rub it in, in wide, circular movements.

Dressed, he looked a little disjointed, as if his business suit was a confinement to him, but now she could see that his proportions were almost classically perfect. His legs and his back were both long, with broad shoulders tapering down to narrow buttocks, and she couldn't help her hands lingering caressingly as she traced the ridges and hollows of his lower spine.

'Mmm,' Brad sighed. He closed his eyes, and she felt the loosening of his muscle tone as he relaxed still further. 'Do my legs as well.'

It felt dangerously intimate to be moving her hands over the hair-roughened surface of his thighs. Brad opened his eyes, a smile twitched the corners of his mouth, and she guessed he was perfectly aware of the effect he was having on her.

That she was having a similar effect on him was obvious when he rolled over on to his back, but he seemed quite unabashed, and otherwise relaxed as she transferred her attentions to his chest.

She curved her hands slightly, letting the sharp tips of her fingernails snag as she ran them over his nipples, and heard the shallow intake of his breath before he said thickly. 'Gently.'

She grinned, exhilarated. 'You like this, don't you?'

'I'd like a whole lot more than this from you.'

'Not here,' Tara retorted, though with a teasing note. She was committed now to taking their relationship further, but for the moment this was pleasure enough— a rich, drugging, sensual pleasure, to have him at her mercy and feel free to stroke, to scratch, to caress. She oiled him all, from the thick column of his neck to the curves of his feet, until he was lying stretched in front of her, gleaming like a bronze statue of a god.

'I hope you're not going to wreck my handiwork by plunging into the sea just yet,' she added.

'Why? Wouldn't you like to do that all over again?' he shot back.

'Later, maybe.'

'Right on. I'm not going to swim yet. I'm so relaxed I don't want to move a muscle.'

'Ooh—and I thought it was my turn now.'

'So it is.' His eyes roamed lazily over the small neat curves of her body. 'Settle down and I'll see about it.'

She copied him, her skin prickling with pleasurable anticipation as she settled on her stomach and laid her cheek against the rough towelling. She couldn't see him, only hear the hiss and rumble of the pebbles shifting as he poised over her, and it felt like a tiny electric shock when the cool trickle of the oil was followed by the confident touch of his fingers.

He was as thorough and attentive to her as she had been to him, letting his hands linger unashamedly in the small of her back, on the soft inner skin of her thighs, on sensitive areas like the inside of her elbows and the back of her knees. His touch wasn't rough, but when he finished she felt as limp as if she had been subjected to an hour-long pummelling by a masseur.

'The sun's not too hot,' Brad murmured, 'so we can afford to sleep.'

'Nice,' Tara whispered back. It was. The sun's warm caress, the soft sound of the sea, the occasional cool tickle of wind against her skin, her easy awareness of Brad by her side, all added up to a recipe for ecstasy.

They sunbathed till midday, when, hot and sticky, she let him persuade her into the sea for the shortest of dips. The water was cold, but she was enchanted by the little fishing village turned resort, with its broad empty vistas of sea and sky.

Lunch was seafood: fried squid, pink juicy prawns and huge portions of sea-bass, followed by gelatinous little sweet cakes made from the local rice crop. Afterwards, hand in hand they explored the medieval fortified church, and climbed its tower. From the top there were impressive views of the flat waste of water and marshland that made up the Camargue, one of the strangest and most impressive natural landscapes in Europe.

Brad talked to her of the famous black bulls and white horses, and of the gypsy population that came each year to perform ceremonies in the church, which was sacred to Sarah, their patron saint; and for a moment she regretted her lazy reluctance to explore the area more fully with him. But the day was perfect in its quiet way, and they spent the rest of the afternoon back on the beach.

It was Tara's turn to talk, now. Brad wanted to know why she had chosen such an unusual career, and she told him about her family, six of them crammed into a smallish house, and the longing that had grown up in her for peace and privacy, a space of her own.

She was the odd one out now among her three sisters, who had all chosen more conventionally feminine jobs. Marie was a secretary, Victoria, a model—much to Brad's amusement, Tara still insisted that she couldn't have imagined doing the same job herself, even if she had been blessed with her sister's height—and Corinne, who was still at school, was planning to work for the local insurance company where her fiancé was a clerk. But Tara didn't mind that, she insisted—she had always been something of a loner. Brad was one, too, she suggested, and he hesitantly agreed.

'But we're talking about you,' he persisted. 'You wanted a solitary job, OK—but why this one?'

'Actually, I think I only discovered slowly that that was what I wanted,' Tara said thoughtfully. 'I started by training in civil engineering—as most of Insco's inspectors do—and I thought of working in the construction industry. I tried that for a year, but I didn't fit. Maybe it was the wrong job, maybe just the wrong firm—I don't know. But then I saw an advert for the Insco job, and I applied on the spur of the moment. So it was happenstance that pushed me towards this career, really—being in the right place at the right time.'

'And will it always mean a lot of travelling?'

'Most likely.' She shrugged. 'When I started, I didn't think in terms of ten, twenty, thirty years on the road. I didn't think, I'm passing up on marriage and a family; I just thought it would be good to travel, now. And it was—it's suited me well. But long-term, if I married, it would be a problem. So many of Insco's inspectors look to switch to desk jobs when they start families, and there aren't enough desk jobs for them all to do.'

'I'll find you plenty to do,' Brad murmured.

'No promises, I thought you said?'

'So I did.' He rolled over to face her, his eyes fixing hers intently. 'But to be honest, I've no doubts—and nor have you, have you?'

At that moment, she hadn't. What she felt for him wasn't just physical attraction, though that was intense enough—it was a feeling of affinity stronger than anything she had ever felt before. She wasn't so blind as to not see that there would be problems, but she felt, just then, a complete conviction that they would overcome them.

The yellow light and long shadows of late afternoon added drama to the eerie landscape as they drove back along the narrow road that crossed the upper reaches of the Camargue, above the restricted area that was kept as a nature reserve. Brad was driving, so Tara could afford to sit back in the luxurious seat of the Ferrari, alternately watching him and the natural beauty that surrounded them.

Mostly, she watched him. It was an intense pleasure to feast her eyes on the harsh line of his profile—the jut of his square chin, shadowed with evening stubble; the tousled mass of his dark hair; the strong arms that wielded the steering-wheel with such confident authority.

She wanted him. He had been right, she thought with quiet amusement, to make her wait. Yesterday she would willingly have made love with him, but today she knew him better, and she wanted him far more. By now she was almost sick with impatience to be in his arms. Every shared glance, every touch throughout that day had served to stoke her longing. And tonight, she felt sure, he would fulfil her every desire.

He took her hand again as they walked from the car

to their hotel, and retrieved their keys from the reception. 'It's almost seven,' Tara said. 'Can you spare me half an hour to shower and change? And we'll meet up again in the bar?'

'No.'

Startled, she turned to look at him.

He smiled, a seductive smile that somehow held both lazy charm, and an undercurrent of hot urgency. 'No, I can't spare you for half an hour,' he amplified, weighing her room key, which he'd taken for her. He turned it in the lock, and guided her before him into her room. . .

And into his arms, for a kiss which told her precisely why he wasn't waiting any longer. He caught her by the waist, and drew her down with him on to the high, lumpy old bed.

'Brad,' Tara breathed. 'We can't——'

His mouth cut off her protest. This kiss, like the last, was hard, confident, sexy. His skin was slicked with the remnants of the tanning oil, and he gave off the musky odour of a sun-warmed male in heat. 'Can't we?' he murmured.

'Well. . .'

He turned on to his back, pulling her gently by the wrist so that she was straddling his big body. 'Why not?' he asked, as his free hand sought out the curves of her breast and waist and hip.

'I can't think when you do that.'

'Don't think, then. Feel. Trust me. Love me.'

His hand on her wrist pulled her down, and slid round her back to hold her close. Her face was level with his, and her feet came to somewhere around his knees—at every point in between, their bodies touched.

Tara sighed. Brad's eyes had darkened till they looked black in the shadows of the room. The white flash of his smile wasn't cowboy any more, it was pure outlaw.

She parted her lips, and lowered her mouth to touch his again—only to have him take over the kiss, intensifying it, accepting her willingness and going on to master her. His tongue was urgent, invading; her breasts, crushed against the solid wall of his chest, were aching with sensation.

When she began to think she could bear it no more, he released her mouth, rolling her over on to her back, and beginning to undo the buttons on her blue cotton blouse. The urgency was still in his movements, but they were controlled now, as if he had dug deep into his reserves, and found the patience necessary to make love to her with subtlety.

One by one, he planted a kiss on each inch of skin as he exposed it. The branding confidence of his mouth, the flirtatious flick of his tongue, the occasional sharp nip from his teeth, had her squirming against him. This was bliss, and yet it was torture, caressing and tormenting, fuelling the ache deep inside her.

His hands found the front catch of her bra and she watched his face, glorying in his fierce concentration, as he released it and replaced the scrap of fabric with the warm caress of his hands. Sturdy artist's thumbs circled each rosy peak, pressing down slightly as her breasts seemed to swell in welcome to him. He flicked her nipples into straining, throbbing awareness, then lowered his head and took first one, then the other, into the warm cavern of his mouth.

Her own hands caressed the firm, smooth skin of his neck and shoulders, reaching down beneath the collar of his shirt. He raised his head to pull it impatiently over his head, and she sighed with pleasure as he replaced it with the electric contact of flesh against flesh.

The rest of their clothes joined their shirts on the floor, as they undressed each other with absorbed urgency. Tara had relished touching and being touched by him that morning, but it was an infinitely more erotic experience now, when they were free to use not only their hands, but their mouths too, and every other part of their bodies.

She dragged her throbbing nipples against his bare chest. She explored his legs with her toes and the soles of her feet, and she planted hot kisses on the faint furrows of his ribs. She slid down the heated length of his body, almost out of reach of his distracting hands, her lips and tongue just reaching out to explore the salty flesh and tangled coarse hair that cradled his maleness, before he groaned and pulled her back, reclaiming her mouth, stealing back the initiative.

He was tense now, and she could feel the dull thud of his heart. She began to sense a languor steal over her, as her original excitement was replaced by a deeper ache of longing. Her body was motionless, unresisting, a column of intensity, as Brad's hands pinned her to the soft mattress.

His hands roved down her body, found the moist core of her longing, and his fingers thrust in a quickening rhythm that heated her to fever pitch.

'Yes. . . Yes!' It was both a sigh of satisfaction, and a plea for more.

'You're so small,' Brad murmured. 'So fragile.'

'Please. . .please. . .'

His hesitation was only momentary. Her voice deserted her, as he moved to position his body over hers. There was a moment, eternal in its tenseness, when she was waiting, focused on the exultant expression on his harshly hewn face, and then he was moving to complete his possession of her.

She was beyond control, beyond waiting. Her body pulsed with waves of pleasure that grew in intensity, till he paused in his movements and she could feel herself clutching at him with hands and womb, then taking off into an explosion of ecstatic fulfilment.

'Yes!' he growled. But the time for relaxation wasn't yet, because he was resuming his own fierce movements, and her body, super-sensitised, rawly attuned to his, eagerly accommodated him as he climbed to the summit of his fulfilment.

He collapsed heavily on her, totally spent, his breath roaring unevenly, and Tara felt herself enfolded as their combined weight pressed down on the yielding mattress.

'I'm too heavy for you,' he apologised when his breath was back, easing off her on to powerful arms, then sliding sideways till he was resting on his back at her side.

'Not really.' She had enjoyed the sensation of being covered by his huge bulk and warm weight, and she moved to curl into his side, not wanting to relinquish him so soon.

'Mmm,' he sighed. 'We're a lot better matched than we look.'

'Perfectly, I'd have said.'

'So would I.' Brad turned his face to her and smiled. 'Five minutes to recover, my love, then I'll leave you to shower, and after that we head for a late supper. OK?'

'I could fall asleep now,' she murmured.

'No chance, honey. The evening's only just begun.'

Tara woke in darkness—woke abruptly, to the strange fierce terror of disorientation. The sheets and the heavy quilt of the bed were warm around her, but for a moment she was chilled almost to shivering. Then her eyes adjusted, and she took in the dimensions of her hotel room in Arles, and the indistinct shape of Brad, a blacker black against the shadows, retrieving his clothes, and slipping them on.

'Urgh,' she groaned. 'What time is it?'

'Five-thirty. Time for me to go.'

She groaned again. It had been eleven when they'd got back to bed, and long after that when they had finally slept. 'So soon?'

'I've to be in Montelimar by eight.' He moved back to the bed, bending his head to give her the lightest of kisses.

But to go—go now! She wouldn't see him again! She'd only just found him, and——

Her arms were reaching for him with something close to panic. This was what she had feared, most of all: that she'd give herself totally to someone, and find them not staying, but stealing away in the dark with her heart.

'Gently, honey,' Brad murmured, taking her wrists and easing them away.

'But. . .but we. . .but I. . .'

'Phone me later, at the factory, and tell me where you're staying. Make it somewhere north of Avignon, if you can. OK?'

'North? But why?'

He gave a cracked laugh. 'You're asleep, aren't you? Why do you think? So I'll get there all the sooner.'

'Oh!' Of course! She'd been thinking she was saying goodbye to him for weeks, perhaps forever—but that wasn't the case at all. She had a couple of assignments near Avignon, as she had already told him, and he'd easily be able to get there from Montelimar.

He laughed again. 'You didn't think I'd just walk out? Honey, that's the last thing I want to do.'

'I hadn't thought. Just that we've so much to sort out, and——'

'Tonight we will,' Brad said firmly. 'Tonight we'll talk properly. But now I've got to get moving.'

'Put the light on.'

'May as well, now you're awake.'

For an instant she had to close her eyes against the brightness, then she opened them a sliver, and watched Brad through her lashes, shrugging on his shirt and buttoning it.

She was aware of her own body too, now—of the reassuring warm ache that brought back the memory of his repeated possession of it, of the heavy weightlessness of arms and legs, of her dry throat and the tangled hair that spread across the bolster.

Brad ran weary fingers through his hair, pushing back his fringe, then glanced around the room as if he were checking for possessions he'd forgotten.

'It's too early for breakfast,' she croaked.

'Yeah. I'll grab some coffee at one of the stops on the *autoroute*.' He stepped towards the door, then paused. 'I'll pay our bill, and breakfast for you. Drive carefully when you go, OK?'

'OK.'

He hesitated for a moment more, then slipped out of the door, and pulled it gently to behind him.

After the honeymoon atmosphere of the weekend, Tara found it doubly wearing to buckle down to work. Fortunately, her day's assignments weren't too demanding. She managed to carry out routine inspections of a couple of small warehouses even when more than half of her mind was on Brad.

She chose a hotel that afternoon with him in mind—
not the city-centre type she would normally have
picked, but a pretty *auberge*, awash with flowers, on a
side-road a few miles outside Avignon. The double bed
was hard by French standards, the en suite shower big
enough for two to share. She curled up on the bed, her
face aglow with anticipation, as she dialled the number
of ECF Montelimar and asked for him.

He was there by seven, striding into their room,
lifting her high for his welcoming kiss, glowing with
joyous confidence.

'Must have been a good day,' Tara teased.

'You think it's work that's got me so happy? Actually
it was—partly,' he agreed, flinging himself down on the
bed. 'It'll take more than one day to get that joint
turned around, but now I've really gotten things in
motion.'

Crisply, confidently, he outlined the day's events to
her. Monsieur Fillol had apparently refused to reinstate
Jean-Claude Morot, complaining that he couldn't work
with a man he didn't trust, and in any case he had
already offered the job to his brother-in-law. It was the
last straw for Brad—he'd promptly fired the general
manager, reinstated Jean-Claude, and offered the manager's job to the deputy manager at ECF's Lyons plant.

'He's young,' Brad explained, 'but he's ambitious. I
told him it was a tough assignment, but he accepted it
right away. I'll stay on for another couple of weeks to
ease him in, but with luck that's one of my biggest
problems solved.'

'I hope so,' Tara agreed. 'It sounds to me as if you
did the right thing, Brad.'

Brad shrugged. 'Firing someone's never a pleasure.
It makes an enemy—this time for you, as well as for
me, since Fillol swore that the incident with you lay

behind it. But sometimes it has to be done, and I guess that was one time it did. Still, let's forget it now. We've got more important things to talk about.'

They ate a simple meal at the *auberge*, and over coffee afterwards Brad launched into their discussion.

'I'll be honest, Tara,' he said. 'My business career's shot ahead over the last few years, but my personal life's gone way off-beam. I hadn't realised how far awry I'd gone, until we met. You told me you thought I was a loner yesterday, and that's true, I suppose, but I wasn't always like that. With Adrienne, my problem was the opposite: I wanted to be too close to her, closer than she could bear.'

'I guess that's no better,' Tara softly suggested.

'Yes and no. It didn't work out, but I think that was mainly because I'd picked the wrong woman. The thing is, I know there's an empty space inside me. I've had a lot of women grumble that I'm stand-offish, I don't get involved enough for them, I don't want them inside my head—and I guess they've been right. I have become like that, since Adrienne and I split. But I don't want to be like that. I'd rather be close to someone, if I can find the right person to be close to. I'd rather have someone fill that space for me.'

'You have,' she assured him.

He nodded. 'Tell the truth, I knew it the first moment I saw you. It scared me sick.'

'Is *that* your excuse?'

'There's no excuse for the way I behaved that first day,' Brad soberly admitted, 'only explanations. But that's the explanation—that, and my fear for you, out in the world alone, doing a lonely job among men who don't always wish you well.'

'It isn't that bad,' Tara complained—but Brad wasn't listening.

'You know what really brought it home to me?' he went on. 'Today, facing up to firing Fillol, I couldn't help thinking of you. A decision like that's never easy to make—and OK, it's mine to make, and I wouldn't ask—wouldn't want—to share it. But once it's made, it makes such a difference to know that I can come home to you, and tell you about it, and have you tell me I made the right choice.'

'You did do right,' Tara assured him.

'Yeah, today I think I did a pretty good job. But whether things have gone right or wrong, what I want is to have you there by my side to share them with. Mine's a tough job, Tara. I've climbed high and fast— but I don't want to climb alone. I want to share it all with you—the successes and the failures, the rewards, the problems—all of it.'

Tara was silent. It wasn't that she was reluctant to reply, just that she was thinking. About Brad, starting out on a new job in a foreign country. Brad working alone, travelling alone, feeling alone.

She loved his power, his decisiveness, his masculinity—but she loved the sensitive side of him, too. Not every man who had risen to head a major organisation at thirty-two would have the courage to see the dark side of the decisions he had to make. Brad had that courage. But if he was to keep rising, and to keep that courage, that integrity, then he needed a woman he could love and trust by his side.

'Tell me you want that too,' he quietly urged her.

'I do, Brad.' She turned shining eyes on him. 'Yes, I do.'

His only answer was to reach out and clasp her hand. They sat there for a moment, silent together, savouring the commitment they had just made.

'I know this is all happening so fast,' Brad said

finally, 'but we're not in a situation where it's easy to go slow. Tomorrow you have to head off back to London, and I wasn't having you go before we'd sorted things out. We'll get married, of course, as soon as we can fix it—but I'd like you to hand in your notice right away. The sooner you get out of that job, the better.'

'Hand in my notice!' Tara exclaimed.

'You have to give a month, do you?'

'I suppose so—but Brad, I can't quit Insco. Not straight away, just like that.'

'Of course you can. They'll miss you, but they'll survive. Insco doesn't need you the way I do.'

'I wasn't thinking of Insco, Brad—I was thinking of me!'

Brad's heavy brows lowered into a frown.

'Darling, be reasonable,' Tara said hastily. 'Of course marrying you is going to mean rethinking my work pattern. I've admitted my job doesn't fit easily with a stable home life, and OK, most likely it'll have to go. But you're asking me to take an enormous step, without giving me a chance to see the way ahead of me. Before I quit Insco, I want to have a feeling for what I should do next.'

'You'll be married to me,' Brad said firmly.

'I know, but darling, that's hardly a full-time occupation! Getting married so fast, we won't want to start a family for a little while—and at least until we do, I'll need a proper job.'

Brad shook his head. 'Tara, you won't—or at least, not the kind of job you have been doing. Believe me. And not only will you not need a job, you simply won't have time to do one.'

'So what will I do? Sit at home and paint my fingernails? Voluntary work in a hospital? Brad, be reasonable! This is the end of the twentieth century!

Maybe a few jet-setting wives don't work, but we'll hardly be in that league! Women like me all work after they marry.'

'You don't understand, Tara. You haven't been to Rouen, to ECF's headquarters. You've only seen me visiting Montelimar—you don't know about my life there. And I'll be making trips to the States three or four times a year at least, and travelling across Europe. I'll want you to be with me, not to be dashing off to inspect some factory on your own.'

'So will I, darling. But think of the other times—the times when you'll be in Rouen, working late, and I'll be stuck at home waiting for you to come back. Think how bored I'll be then! All right, I want to be your wife and your support, Brad, but I want to be your partner, not your puppet!'

'You will be. But you can't be, if you carry on working for Insco.'

She sighed. 'You really hate my job, don't you?'

'That's too strong a word,' Brad said. 'I don't hate fire protection, Tara. What I hate is the thought of you travelling, being away when I want you near. I hate the thought of you working in factories with strange men. That's what I won't have, and the only way to stop that, as far as I can see, is for you to stop working for Insco.'

'Maybe. But—Brad, all right, we're both making a quick decision to marry, but it seems that it's me who has to make all the changes. You're asking me to leave my home country, my family, my friends, my job, in favour of a place I've never seen, and a lifestyle I just can't imagine suiting me. It's too much to ask, all at once.'

'But what's the alternative? What's the point of

taking time over the decision, when we'd have to spend that time apart?'

'We wouldn't necessarily,' Tara assured him. 'Insco are quite civilised—they do give me holidays! And this isn't the only work I'll ever do in France. If I ask Jim, perhaps he'll give some more French assignments over the next few months. Who knows? I could inspect your Rouen headquarters.'

'Seriously? Do you think you could?'

'It's worth trying.'

They discussed the possibilities for the remainder of the evening. In spite of his earlier stance, Brad did make an effort not to be too inflexible. Working for Insco wouldn't be at all practicable after they married, he insisted to Tara; but he agreed that it might make sense for her to carry on her work during their engagement, especially if she could arrange to spend some of her time with him.

Then she would see Rouen, and gain more of a feeling for the lifestyle that she was to share. Then she would have a chance to consider whether and how she might pursue her career in a slightly different way after their marriage. And then—although she didn't say this out loud to him—she'd have a chance to develop his trust in her, and repair some of the damage that the breakdown of his marriage had caused.

about. If you were at my last hotel, I'd send you there
in December.'

'I wouldn't mind,' Tara said, 'the snow.' Tara noticed

It's a great sight at night, all iced the mail.

was a great sight at night, all iced she

'When did you last see it . . .'

CHAPTER SIX

'HI, PETE. Hi, Joe. Yes, just back from France—had
a great time.'

Tara breezed along the corridor of Insco's London
office, greeting the inspectors who were currently desk-
based, and pausing to chat with a few as she made her
way to Jim Backley's office.

Jim was on the phone when she peeped round his
door, but he motioned to her to come in. She grinned
at him, pleased to see the grizzled old engineer again,
then settled down in his spare chair and glanced around
as she waited for him to finish his call.

On the wall of his office, which was utilitarian rather
than smart, was posted a large chart marking the
location of each member of Jim's field force of inspectors. Tara squinted across at it, realised he had written
it up a couple of months ahead, and crossed to check
her own entries.

The stint in southern France that she had just completed was marked, then a short gap when presumably
she would be occupied in the office, reviewing other
inspectors' reports; then Jim had her down to inspect a
huge electronics factory in Norway, followed by half a
dozen smaller plants there and just over the Swedish
border.

'Yep,' Jim said, setting down the receiver. 'I had a
blitz on the scheduling last week, fixed you all up right
through till the end of July.'

'You want me to go to Bergen?'

'Smile, love. Norway in June; what's that to grouch

about? If you were in my bad books I'd send you there in December.'

'I wouldn't mind, I like the snow,' Tara retorted. 'It's a good assignment, Jim—but to tell the truth, I was hoping to get back to France.'

'What's this, your love-life?'

'Something like that.'

'You got holidays for that, love.'

'I know, but—well, no harm in asking.'

'You've cleared up round Avignon, in any case. There's nothing more scheduled there till September.'

'There are other parts of France.'

'Hey, how far are you prepared to go to see this guy?'

'Actually he's based in Rouen—ECF's head-quarters.'

'Ah, ECF. So you're falling for the clients now.'

'Singular, Jim,' Tara said tartly. 'Only one client.'

Jim frowned, and tapped the blunt end of his biro on his notepad. 'What's his job?'

'European director.'

He whistled, soundlessly, then frowned again, then said in a thoughtful voice, 'So that cuts out all the ECF initial inspections.'

'Does it?'

'Tara, love, how long have you worked for me?'

'Long enough to know the rules.' She mooched from chart to chair, sat, slumped back, and eyed Jim with a mixture of belligerence and defiance. 'But he's not in direct charge of the security precautions at any of the plants, and I thought maybe you'd trust me to be objective enough to——'

'Yep, objective when the ratings are good, but what happens when you hit an unreliable fire pump?'

'Then I lean on him to get it put right. He's on our side, after all.'

'Till he's fathoming out his budget priorities,' Jim said sourly. 'Anyway, you have to look at the other angle. Maybe he reckons when that happens he'll be in a position to lean on you.'

'But I know my job, and I'm not open to leaning on.'

'Yep, I know, but does this guy know that?'

'For heaven's sake, Jim, if you're suggesting——'

'I am,' Jim interrupted. 'OK, Tara, you're starry-eyed, but I can tell you I've seen it all before. You wouldn't be the first inspector to be seduced by a good-looking boss or a pretty secretary, who ended up being persuaded that their readings were awry, or the water pressure had hit an unexpected low on the day of their test.'

'I'd have thought you'd trust me more than that.'

'I've trusted people before and been let down,' Jim said grimly. 'Look, I'm not saying this guy's picked you up in the hope of getting a favourable report—though that's happened before, more than once—but I am saying he most likely reckons your falling for him won't do his insurance rates any harm. I'll trust you as far as I think's reasonable, but I'm warning you, don't you trust him any further than that.'

'So it's a case of no can do.'

'No can swap Bergen, love. The files are on your desk already. I'll have a think about what you should do after that.'

'I'd be glad if you did. I've a couple of weeks' holiday in early September in any case, but if I could combine that with a bit of work almost anywhere in France. . .'

'Then I'll have an inspector resigning to get married or something.'

'I don't know about the "or something",' she teased.

'But I'll tell you one thing, Jim—I'm much more likely to resign if you don't oblige me than if you do.'

'That's what they all say. OK, skedaddle. You've got the Bergen files to read through, then there's a pile of reports to review.'

'I've got my Avignon reports still to finish first.'

'Should have done that yesterday,' he grouched.

'Slave-driver!' Tara groaned—but she was smiling as she closed his office door behind her. Jim's bark might be loud but he wasn't a biter, and she guessed that if she did a good job of the Scandinavian work, he would dig her out something in France for the autumn.

So she'd got about what she'd expected out of him, but that was a great deal less, she knew, than Brad had expected.

Their discussion over, Brad had begun to talk as if it would only be days before she was back in France. How could it be, though? She would certainly try to get across to Paris for the occasional quick weekend, but beyond that, work had to take priority.

Brad wouldn't like that. But he'd grin and bear it, surely, just as she would do. And when the rest of her life was at stake, she knew she was being sensible in treading carefully, and waiting to discover what she was committing herself to, before she made any irrevocable moves.

Once she was caught up with the Bergen inspection, Tara found it hard to spare the time to write long letters to Brad; and he was equally busy, to judge from the scrawled postcards she received from points north, south, east and west of France. But they made up for the dearth of letters with a succession of wickedly expensive phone-calls, and in the middle of July they did better than that, as Brad awarded himself a long weekend, and took a Friday evening flight to Bergen airport.

Tara was waiting in the Arrivals Hall, and a long wait it was too, since his plane was delayed, but finally the passengers began to trickle through Customs, and she saw his tall, rangy figure emerge and stop to search the hangar-like building for her.

For a moment she just stood watching him. He was tanned much more deeply than he had been five weeks earlier, and he looked fit and relaxed. But there was still an air of command about him, which had several people turning to look, as if they half thought they recognised his tall figure.

His eyes flicked over the crowd of people in which she stood, then jerked back to her, and his face lit up in a smile of dazzling pleasure.

'Hi, darling. I——' Tara began.

She hadn't a chance to say more, because he'd dropped his bag and caught her up, lifting her clear off the floor and whirling her around before pulling her close, dizzy, to claim their first kiss in weeks.

'I thought it'd be cold up here,' he commented, as they retrieved her hire car, and he found himself rapidly shedding a heavy pullover.

'No, they usually have a lovely summer. Long light evenings and hot afternoons.'

'Any chance of a swim?'

'Now here the water *is* cold. Remember Les Saintes-Maries-de-la-Mer?'

'How could I forget it?'

'Imagine water twice as cold as that, and you've got the Hardanger Fiord in July.'

'But it's all right for swimming otherwise, is it?'

'Where we're staying you can swim, apparently. The plant manager recommended the hotel to me—it's on the edge of the fiord, about thirty miles inland from here. There won't be beaches, but there's swimming from jetties, and there are some good walks in the mountains.'

'And a double bed.'

'With a hard Scandinavian mattress,' she agreed, laughing.

She was light-hearted with delight as Brad folded his long body into the little car, and they set off through the spectacular upland scenery, and down to the shore of the huge fiord. Brad had never been to Norway before, and soon they were in fits of laughter as she tried to teach him the few words of the language that she had picked up—although, as she assured him, in the tourist resorts almost everybody spoke English.

The hotel that the plant manager had recommended turned out to be small but charming, a collection of log cabins grouped around the shore of the fiord. Their room looked out over the water to the mountains opposite, some of the higher ones snow-capped even in midsummer.

'Great view,' Brad murmured.

'I thought you came for the view of me, not the mountains,' Tara teased.

'That's what I meant, idiot!'

She pushed at him playfully, and he fell on to the bed, pulling her with him.

'Ah, it's great to see you again,' he sighed, as they surfaced from a long, involved kiss. 'But it's been too long, Tara—three weeks since we met up in Paris. And that was only for two days—and this is only for three. I know I said I'd put up with you working for a while, but I never realised we'd see as little of each other as we do.'

'I know, darling, but I've some good news about

that. I didn't want to tell you till it was definite, but Jim confirmed it yesterday. Second half of August, he's scheduling me work in western France. Including, guess what?'

'ECF?' Brad hazarded.

'The Rouen headquarters, *and* the warehouse in Louviers.'

'That's great!'

'Isn't it?' she beamed. She had spent half an hour tussling with Jim over the phone, *and* threatened an immediate resignation, before he'd given in—but she didn't want to tell Brad that. 'All in all I should have three weeks' work within reach of Rouen, plus my fortnight's holiday, so I'll be there for five weeks in total.'

'It's just what we wanted,' Brad agreed. 'A chance for you to find out what life in Rouen's like—and that you won't be bored silly if you give up work.'

'I'd say,' Tara retorted, 'that it was a chance for *you* to discover that I really can combine work with caring for you. After all, I will be working, darling, for most of the time I'm there.'

'But it won't be anything like your travelling.'

'True. And while I'm over there I'll find time to look around and see if there are any jobs going that might suit me better.'

'I'd rather you stopped work altogether, but that would be better than nothing. We can't go on for much longer as we are, Tara. At the end of that five weeks I want you to quit Insco for good, and marry me.'

'You're right,' she agreed. 'We can't go on like this.' She wanted to be with Brad, and for the kind of happiness she felt now to last all the time. But would she be happy, leading the kind of life that he seemed to want her to lead? That was a question she still couldn't answer to her own satisfaction.

Tara arrived in Rouen, the sprawling capital of upper Normandy, at three o'clock on a dull, rainy afternoon—and spent another hour failing to make heads or tails of the horrendous one-way system before she managed to find a car park within reasonable reach of ECF's headquarters in the centre of the city.

Then came an umbrella-and-briefcase-laden dash along the banks of the majestic River Seine. This quarter of the city had largely been rebuilt after the war, and she had read up some preliminary details of the locations she was to inspect, so she already knew that the ECF Building was a towering block of concrete and glass.

Such a posh block, though! Definitely thriving-international-corporation, she decided, dashing under the entrance canopy, and gratefully lowering her umbrella. Everything about it spoke of money and power, from the glass doors twice her height, to the array of lifts, to the plush-looking reception area with orange carpets and huge tubs of plants.

Of course ECF was a sizeable outfit, while SHP, the American company that had taken it over, was vast even by global standards. She knew that; she'd known it since long before she'd met Brad Hamilton. She'd known he was successful, and obviously well off. But it struck her now, uneasily, that she hadn't really considered just what his Rouen lifestyle was like.

It was quite possible, she supposed, that the boss of *this* outfit really would expect to have the kind of fashion-plate wife who spent her time socialising and doing 'good works', soothing his tired brow, and charming his clients.

That wasn't Brad, though. Surely it wasn't! Brad was the man who'd bummed around Paris trying to paint, a bare six years earlier. Brad had fallen in love with her, a career-orientated woman—a virago, even!—and not with an insipid model-type. He might be rich and powerful, but she was still her own woman, and not to be bulldozed into doing anything that wasn't right for her.

But. . .it wouldn't just be Brad against her. This whole formidable organisation would try to mould her into a shape that suited it, if she married him. The boss's wife. She sneaked another glance through the glass doors at the fearsomely chic receptionist manning the marble and steel desk, and wondered how *she* would picture the boss's wife.

Doubtless she wouldn't have pictured anyone looking quite like Tara at that moment, the boss's fiancée thought to herself, glancing ruefully down at her rain-spattered figure. And it wasn't just the rain. Attractive she might be, but she didn't have the gloss, the poise, the immense self-confidence that surrounded rich men's women. Her navy-blue suit was smart, but it was inspecting-factories smart, not supper-at-Maxim's smart. Hers was a working girl's simple grooming, her hairstyle and make-up chosen for easy maintenance, rather than to impress.

So? She might not look the part, but she *was* the boss's fiancée, and it wouldn't do her any good indulging in a fit of nerves now!

A smile tweaked the corners of her mouth, as she pushed open the heavy glass doors. 'Mr Hamilton, *s'il vous plaît*,' she said sweetly to the aloof receptionist. 'Yes,' she added in English. 'He is expecting me.'

So he was. There was her name, on the receptionist's appointment list. And if the receptionist thought that

Tara's outfit looked as if it came from a chain store—
which it did—or that her pony-tail was lacking in high
style, she had more tact than to show it. She was
politeness personified as she ushered Tara to the private lift—*private lift*!—that led up to the European
director's office on the top floor.

When the lift doors slid open after a breathlessness-
inducing whizz upwards, another chic Frenchwoman—
this one blonde, tall, and reed thin—was already
waiting to greet her. Then there was barely time to
relocate the stomach she felt she'd left twenty floors
down, before she was ushered into Brad's office. And
there he was, right in front of her.

Her stomach vanished again, and her throat tightened. If his office had seemed forbidding, the man
himself knocked her for six.

For an instant she didn't recognise her lover at all in
the tall figure that uncurled from behind half an acre of
mahogany desk. From his immaculately cut charcoal
suit to his hightly polished black shoes, he was every
inch a captain of industry. This didn't seem like the
man she'd pushed into the icy waters of the Hardanger
Fiord a few weeks earlier—this was a man who
belonged in these daunting surroundings. Powerful,
commanding, it was easy to tell that he controlled
millions of pounds and hundreds of men.

She faltered. There was a sickening instant when she
felt she had made the most awful mistake in coming.
Then a familar smile creased Brad's face and softened
the line of that implacable jaw. He moved forward to
take her hands in his.

'Darling,' he said in a husky voice. 'You found it all
right?'

Tara's insides creaked back to something like their

normal places. 'It'd be hard to miss,' she wryly acknowledged.

'And you've met Juliette, my personal assistant?'

Automatically, Tara glanced behind her at the blonde woman. There was just an instant when she thought she saw the trace of a scowl on Juliette's perfectly made-up face, then the impression vanished, and Juliette was moving forwards with a courteous smile.

'So I have.'

'You've had a long journey? Like some coffee? Juliette, could you. . .?'

'Certainly.'

'Thank you,' Tara said. '*Café au lait*, please, with no sugar.'

Juliette closed the door behind her, and for a moment Tara and Brad were alone.

Her eyes swept from the closed door through which she had watched Juliette depart, via a vista of rain-darkened roofs seen through plate glass, to Brad's face. She found his eyes, recognised the smile that lit their depths, and knew, suddenly, that everything was going to be all right.

'Overwhelming, isn't it?' he said softly.

'Just a bit.'

'The French like the grand style. You soon get used to it. And there's a great view; come and see.'

His hand, light on her shoulder, drew her across to the window. Still holding her by his side, he outlined the sights to her—the silver ribbon that was the Seine; the pitched roofs of the old town; the soaring spire of the cathedral. Though he had lived there only a few months, he seemed to know Rouen well, and affection for the place thickened his voice.

They barely registered the reappearance of Juliette

with a tray of coffee and biscuits. Brad's assistant had
to rattle the cups loudly to draw his attention; and
Tara, turning round in the same movement as his,
couldn't imagine now why she had found her surroundings intimidating. Certainly the office was vast, and
expensively furnished in a very formal antique style—
but it felt already as if she, like Brad, had grown into
it.

'Thanks, Juliette,' Brad said casually.

'That'll be all, sir?'

'Sure will.'

'Don't forget you've Monsieur Cavaillon coming to
see you at five.'

'I'm not likely to, honey.'

'Shall I switch the phone through to my desk?'

'Yeah, answer it until Miss Miller goes.'

Juliette hovered for a moment, then glided to the
door. As she closed it Tara turned to Brad, frowning.

She hadn't come to the office to start her insurance
inspection—she planned to do that at the end of her
Rouen schedule, in three weeks' time. She had come
because Brad had suggested that she meet up with him
there. And he had promised to leave work early so that
he could take her back to his apartment.

'I know,' Brad said huskily.

'You can't get away.'

'No, dammit.' He reached out and pulled her to him,
setting hands on her waist and drawing her upwards as
he bent down until her mouth was within reach of his.

His kiss was hard, sexy, but reassuring, as was the
hand that ran possessively down the curves of her side
before sliding round to cup her buttocks.

'Can I wait for you?'

'Wait here, you mean? Better not to, I reckon. You
must be tired, and it could take a while.'

'Who's Cavaillon?'

'The new manager at Montelimar, the one who replaced Fillol.' He released her gently. 'He's going back down there in the morning, and I couldn't find another time to see him.'

'That's a pity.'

'How true. It's a tough initiation into how things are gonna be. Much as I'd like to spend all my time with you, I've this damned outfit to run, and it sure takes some running.'

'I know, darling. I'd just hoped that——'

'So'd I. Hell, you know how much I've missed you. Up till yesterday I had this whole afternoon free, but I might have guessed it was too much to aim for.'

'Oh, well.' She didn't want to play too heavily on her disappointment, so she crossed to pick up her coffee-cup, and used the distraction as a chance to recover her equanimity. 'I guess I can find my way, if you show me on a map.'

'No need. I've fixed for Juliette to take you to the apartment.'

'Oh?'

He must have seen the flicker of annoyance that accompanied her surprise, but he didn't mention it. 'It's probably best if you go fairly soon,' he continued. 'The rush-hour tends to start early here. You'll have time to shower and relax, then we'll go out to eat when I get back. That won't be much after six, I hope.'

'Dare I ask you to make that a promise?'

'If you don't think I'm aching to get you alone. . .'

'I wouldn't have come, darling.' She had to kick-start her smile, but it spread effortlessly as Brad took her cup out of her hands, and pulled her back into his arms.

'That's just a taster,' he murmured, after a kiss that

did everything to waken her appetite for more, 'to be followed up the moment I can manage it.'

'Now that,' Tara responded, 'I will take as a promise!'

Juliette, receiving Tara from Brad at his office door, looked no more enthusiastic about his arrangement than Tara herself felt. She obviously wasn't the kind of secretary who felt it necessary to ingratiate herself with the boss's wife. Or maybe she didn't expect Tara really to become his wife, Tara thought to herself.

Or perhaps it wasn't policy, but just a jealousy that Juliette couldn't manage to hide. After all, Brad was very eligible—and coming to work for him as a single man, his secretary might well have had ambitions of her own. Juliette wasn't pretty, but her poise and elegance made her extremely attractive in a sophisticated way. *She* was definitely the rich man's wife type.

The lift arrived, and Juliette briskly punched the button for the basement.

'Why the basement?' Tara asked.

'That's where the car park is.'

'Actually, I didn't park there; Brad didn't tell me there was one. I'm in the public car park on the Quai Pierre Corneille.'

'My car's in our car park. We can go in that.'

'Thank you, but I'd rather not leave mine in the city centre. Will it be a problem for you getting back if we take my car?'

'I can call a taxi,' Juliette said coldly.

They emerged at the lobby. The rain had almost stopped as they began to walk the couple of blocks to the car park.

'Brad's apartment is outside the city, isn't it?' Tara asked, to break the uncomfortable silence.

'About ten kilometres away.'

Juliette's cool tones didn't encourage more questions, and Tara didn't try to ask any.

In any case, there was little more opportunity to chat on the way to the apartment, as the traffic in the city centre was already building up. Juliette's directions were clear and concise, but it took all Tara's concentration to negotiate the unfamiliar crowded roads.

She knew already that Brad lived in a small village up-river, in an apartment overlooking the Seine, but she hadn't asked him any more about it. No problem, though—Juliette knew her way perfectly. She knew just where to turn into the narrow car park entrance, which way the key turned in the lock, which way it was to the living area, and to the kitchen, and to Brad's bedroom.

And she made sure that Tara noticed, Tara thought grouchily. Tara wasn't the jealous type, and she'd never really worried that Brad might have looked elsewhere while she was working away from France; after all, if he'd fallen for his secretary he would hardly have bothered to pursue her! But she had a nasty suspicion that she might *need* to act more possessively towards him, if she was to give Juliette a strong enough keep-off message.

At first sight, the apartment was larger and more luxurious than she had expected—even though she had expected it to be fairly impressive—but she wasn't giving Juliette the pleasure of realising that. She confined her comments to the occasional nod, and an agreement that the view was lovely, then offered to phone for a taxi for Juliette.

'I'll do that,' Juliette coolly corrected her.

There was an awkward fifteen-minute interval before the taxi arrived. Tara didn't want more coffee, and she didn't like to take her suitcase into Brad's room and begin to unpack while Juliette was there. She invited the other woman to sit down in the living area—although Juliette was acting almost as if it should be she who issued the invitations, she thought, with irritation—and they carried on a limping conversation about Rouen's tourist attractions.

It was a relief when the doorbell rang, and Juliette rose to go.

'I expect I'll see you again,' Tara said politely, forcing a smile.

'I'm sure you will.'

Worse luck, Tara thought wearily, closing the front door with a sigh of relief.

Why did women have to be so bitchy to each other? Why all the endless little power struggles, as if life was about nothing more than getting a man, keeping a man, fighting off other women who wanted your man? Thank goodness her life *wasn't* like that! She loved Brad, but she didn't want to lose her own identity, and become nothing more than Mrs Brad Hamilton. If she did do that, she could well imagine she would soon start becoming paranoid about Juliette.

How gruesome it would be to mooch about this big empty apartment all day, knowing Brad was closeted with Juliette, waiting only for him to come home—late, most likely, after yet another last-minute urgent meeting. How much better to have her own life, her own work, other things to keep her interest. Brad might not want that, but surely that was the only way in which they would be able to carry on a reasonably equal relationship.

Although to be fair, there wasn't much equality between them now, she thought uneasily. Her career was going well, but she didn't have anything approaching his wealth and power. She guessed it would be an uphill struggle to maintain her own side of the equation, when the full weight of ECF was ranged against her.

Brad wouldn't have been Brad, though, if he hadn't been a success in life. She couldn't imagine, either, falling in love with a man who was a failure, or tying her own destiny to someone without a clear sense of where he was going. It was just that *she* wanted to know where she was going, too.

He needed to appreciate that, or else she guessed that they would be doomed to disaster. But how was she to bring it home to him?

Oh, well, that problem would have to wait. She drifted back into the living area. It was a huge open space, with a wall of glass looking out across the river. Decorator-designed, she guessed—it had the sort of artistic clutter that Brad couldn't conceivably have accumulated in a few short months. It was attractive and welcoming, but almost *too* perfect, as if nobody had really lived there much.

A seating area defined by three big squashy sofas dominated the room, though there were other smaller groupings of chairs that she could just imagine the decorator positioning to the inch. Antique rugs brightened the polished floorboards. A welcoming array of plants included a couple of palms that stretched almost to the ceiling, and on the walls there were shelves containing leather-bound books, an expensive-looking stereo system and compact discs, and a number of oil paintings that looked, mercifully, as if they hadn't come from the nearest corporate-art-for-investment specialist.

They were the nicest things in the room. She crossed over to look at the nearest one, a street scene—of

Paris, she guessed—that burst with the vitality and individuality which the rest of the room lacked.

Paris. Had Brad bought this when he had lived there?

No—of course! He'd been a painter when he lived in Paris, so what more natural than that he should still possess some of his own work?

She moved closer, searching for a signature, and was rewarded by discovering the initials 'BCH' scrawled in the bottom right-hand corner. That proved it—it had to be his.

So this was the failed painter's work? This was what the spoilt rich-kid had wasted his time doing? You idiot, Brad Hamilton! she felt like screaming. Your work's marvellous!

Of course she wasn't an art expert, but she had confidence in her own taste, and she knew from experience that what she liked was generally popular with others, too. She couldn't be wrong in finding it good. Brad used colour and line boldly and effectively, and the composition was as strong as it was simple.

With mounting enthusiasm she toured around the apartment, looking at the rest of the pictures. Many of the others were also Parisian scenes, most of them similar in style to the first she'd seen. A handful of landscapes not in Brad's distinctive style had, she guessed, been painted by friends of his, and over his bed was a picture showing a group of people, including a younger version of Brad himself. He was sitting in a café, looking relaxed and long-legged in denims and a white open-necked shirt, a glass of beer in one hand.

It wasn't a particularly good picture, but it gave off a good atmosphere, of happiness and relaxation and camaraderie. It was the sort of painting that made you wish you were there, sitting in that café, young and carefree, and having a great time.

That had been Brad, once; that had been his life. For seven years he'd lived in Paris, had a good time with friends, and thrown himself into producing the glorious paintings that hung all over this apartment. And then he'd left it all behind him.

That decision had sounded so simple, so right, when he'd told her his story in Arles—but it couldn't really have been like that, she thought now. From the way he kept his work on display, she guessed he'd never completely managed to persuade himself that he was untalented. It must have wrenched him to the soul to give up on his dream of becoming a great artist, and go to work for the family firm instead.

And what had happened to the family firm? The obligation that he'd felt then must have proved to be a mirage, presumably, if he'd left it behind him so rapidly. So in truth, he'd abandoned his painting for what? A new Ferrari? A plushly impersonal apartment in Rouen?

It struck her, right then, as the lousiest of bargains.

Did Brad secretly think so too?

All sorts of ideas were swarming into her head, all sorts of possibilities opening up. Too many—and she was too tired to think them through properly. Anyway, they needed to be discussed with Brad, rather than provide the basis for solitary fantasies. With an effort she turned away from the café painting, and towards her unpacked suitcase.

By now she had begun to feel at ease in the apartment, and she soon relaxed enough to take literally Brad's invitation to make herself at home. She poured herself a long weak gin and tonic, put a jazz record on the stereo, and began to hum along with the infectious rhythm as she hung her working suits in the wardrobe space she guessed he had cleared specially for her.

CHAPTER SEVEN

'TOMORROW,' Brad said decisively, 'I'll cook supper for you.'

'There's no need, darling. I know you work hard, and it's no disgrace to go to restaurants after a long day at the office.'

'I'll do it Saturday, then.'

'OK,' Tara agreed, 'and I'll cook us Sunday lunch.'

'Are you any good?'

'I'm well trained; usually competent, occasionally inspired. At home we all took it in turns to do supper, and the comments were pretty harsh if we didn't make a good job of it.'

'I bet.'

'How about you?' she asked.

'Oh, I never cooked at home, nor much in Paris, come to that. I really learned to cook when I got back to the States, and found myself missing French food. The ingredients are first-rate back home, but they don't put them together in the same way. So I messed around at the weekends, bought a cook-book or two——'

'I noticed the shelf-full in the kitchen.'

'—and a store of herbs. Garlic too, I love garlic.'

'Great. What'll you cook on Saturday?'

'Maybe a chicken Norman-style, baked in cider and served with a cream sauce.'

'I can hardly wait.'

'Oh, it's so good to have you here!' Brad rolled over on to his side and hugged her to him, then caught his hands in the tangled mass of her hair and eased her head back so that he could kiss her again.

Tara stirred and moved her body sensuously against his. They had already made love once, but she could easily have been persuaded to start all over again.

'Yes,' Brad whispered, dropping light kisses on the curve of her shoulder, 'but if we do that now we'll be too late for supper.'

'And you're hungry.'

'Always am. There's a lot of me to feed. Hungry for you, too, but I've taken the edge off that appetite for now.' He released her abruptly, flung back the duvet that covered them, and swung his legs out of bed. 'Want to shower?' he went on.

'After you will do fine.'

'With me would do better.'

'I thought you wanted to hurry out to supper!'

'Well. . .' catching her hand, and pulling her after him '. . .maybe not that much of a hurry!'

It was almost eight o'clock when they finally made their way out of the apartment, and down the road to a little restaurant in the centre of the village. Brad had changed into casual trousers and a yellow shirt, and seemed much more like the man Tara had known in Montelimar than the industrialist who had briefly intimidated her that afternoon.

'Hey,' she said, over their aperitifs, 'I love your paintings.'

'Do you?' He grinned, almost boyishly. 'That's good.'

'You should do some more.'

'No time, honey.'

'No, seriously, Brad. You've such talent—I hate to think of you never using it again.'

He shrugged. 'That's life. I told you, Tara, I need all

my energy to set ECF to rights. I've never been able to see painting as relaxation, so I won't do it as a hobby. It has to be all or nothing, and I chose to make it nothing.'

'Don't you regret that sometimes?'

'I can't say I do. I like my job. There are times when the problems just about drive me crazy, but basically I love it. I like being stretched, and I'm lucky—I've been promoted fast enough that I've always found my work a challenge.'

'I can see that, but. . .oh, forget it. I'm just sorry you're not painting any more. When I think of some of those views in the Camargue, and what you might have made of those. . .'

'That'll have to wait till I retire,' Brad said lightly. 'Now, what shall we eat?'

Tara didn't persist, dropping the subject and joining him in studying the menu. The evening of their reunion wasn't the time to push him any harder. But, underneath the more casual chat that filled the rest of the evening, her mind continued to work away at the thought of Brad's painting.

'OK, let it flow.'

Jacques Michelet, manager of ECF's Louviers warehouse, nodded dourly, his mouth working hard on the piece of gum he had been chewing ever since Tara had arrived. He began to turn the wrench he had fitted on to the water valve, and, first in a rusty trickle, then in a clean gush, the water spilled out and across the warehouse yard.

'Enough?' Michelet shouted over the roar.

'Is that full on?'

'Almost.'

'Take it right to the last turn.'

Michelet wrenched again, then straightened himself. 'That's all.'

Tara frowned. Was it? Then she guessed it wasn't enough. This warehouse had a sprinkler system, but it didn't have a fire pump and water storage tank—the system was fed straight from the mains. It took an exceptional water pressure to handle that kind of demand, and this didn't look to be any more than average.

Still, it wasn't her job to guess, not when accurate answers were there for the taking. She moved to the back of the hydrant, out of range of all but the odd spatter, and leaned forward so that she could position her pitot tube in mid-flow.

'What's that?'

'It's for testing the water pressure.' She glanced round, meaning to explain to Michelet, but his interest obviously wasn't great enough for him to risk getting wet.

She angled the tube so that its holes received the full force of the water, leaned a little further over, and read the pressure off the attached gauge. Then she drew back, nodded to Michelet that he could turn off the valve now, and picked up her clipboard so that she could note down the reading.

'That's finished?' Michelet asked.

'This hydrant is. I'll have to test the other hydrant too, and then run some water from the end of the sprinkler pipe run.'

'Our old insurers never did this.'

'Then they didn't have Insco's scientific approach to fire protection. We're famed for it. We don't simply collect premiums, we provide a total fire protection service—and we give very large discounts to well-protected properties.'

Michelet paused in his wrenching and shrugged, as if this information meant nothing to him. Perhaps it didn't, Tara thought. He didn't seem to be a lively man, or interested in anything beyond his own narrow responsibilities.

He did his job well, though—the warehouse was clean and orderly, just about the exact opposite of Montelimar. That factory had had good fire protection, but bad management; in this place the management was good, but the fire protection poor.

Deceptively poor, at that; inadequately fed sprinklers only instilled a false sense of security.

The stupidity of it, she thought, with familiar anger. The sprinkler system must have cost thousands of pounds, but what use was all that agglomeration of pipework and valves, unless it delivered sufficient water to put out a fire?

In storage like this, plastic bathroom accessories packed in several layers of cardboard, any fire would spread within seconds. Maybe thirty sprinklers would be triggered in the first five minutes, and the ones furthest along the pipe run wouldn't send out even a trickle!

It would be all too easy for a fire to engulf the entire warehouse. There was no option—she would have to recommend that a proper fire pump be installed.

She followed Michelet to the second hydrant, then checked the water piping that supplied the sprinklers. Then she withdrew to a corner of the small warehouse office, got out her calculator, and started to calculate what size of pump and tank would be needed.

Michelet came back into the office just as she was finishing.

'So? We pass?' he asked.

'It's not a question of passing or failing,' Tara quietly

explained. 'It's a question of grading the protection system—and to tell the truth, yours isn't adequate right now. I'll have to check with my Head Office before I make any official recommendations, but I can tell you already that you're going to need a fire pump and tank.'

'A tank? Why? You saw, there's plenty of water.'

'Not really, there isn't. It may look like lots when you see it gushing out of a hydrant, but allow for the pressure loss in taking it up to the roof and through those narrow pipe lengths, allow for a large area of sprinklers operating simultaneously, and it just won't suffice.'

Michelet spread his hands in resignation—and Tara barely suppressed a sigh. She explained to him at greater length, but he evidently wasn't mathematically-minded enough to follow her calculations, and he still didn't seem convinced.

Oh, well. Michelet wouldn't be the man to authorise the expenditure—that would be Michel Guerard, manager of ECF's western region. He'd surely appreciate her arguments, and if he didn't agree, she could always depend upon Brad to get her recommendations carried out.

After thanking Michelet for his co-operation, she loaded her papers and tools back into her car. It was almost five o'clock—time to go home.

Well, to Brad's apartment, but that was already coming to feel like home to her. She and Brad got on so well, living together. In nearly three weeks they had only had one argument—although that one had been a humdinger, and it hadn't been resolved when she had left that morning. What was more, she had probably made it worse, she thought ruefully, by staying on to reason with Michelet.

Brad had been so insistent that she should get back

to Rouen by six that evening. He needed her to help entertain his clients, he'd claimed, and after putting up with her arriving late for three or four earlier client dinners, he'd chosen to make an issue out of this one.

Tara had thought—still thought—that it was unreasonable of him. She hadn't arrived all that late on the earlier occasions; admittedly, she'd missed a couple of drinks in the boardroom, but each time she had got there well before they moved on to a restaurant. If she hadn't been in Rouen he'd have managed without her, after all.

He'd have managed with Juliette, actually.

And to be fair, she hadn't the remotest wish to miss out while he and Juliette entertained clients together. But while she was working for Insco, her assignments had to come before Brad's clients and their fancy dinners.

Of course it was a problem. She knew it was a problem. But there wasn't any easy solution to it.

Something had to give, between his job and hers; she knew that perfectly well. But what? She still couldn't see herself throwing up work and being contented as a housewife-cum-hostess to Brad, and her preliminary enquiries hadn't brought to light any alternative jobs she might do in Rouen.

Anyway, why did it have to be she who made all the sacrifices? It could have been Brad who gave way. She still half believed he secretly wished he could abandon his business career and return to painting. But when she had very tentatively raised this suggestion he had reacted with contempt, telling her she didn't understand him at all.

Privately, she suspected he didn't understand himself, but it wouldn't have been a sensible tactic to tell him so to his face.

She would be able to limit the short-term damage, she knew, by rushing back to the apartment, changing as fast as she could, and dashing on to the ECF Head Office. But the underlying problem would still be there. Within the remaining two weeks of her stay in France, she and Brad needed to sort out a pattern of life and work that would suit them both—and they were a long way away from achieving that.

Tonight, though, they would have to bury their differences in front of Brad's clients. She swung the car into the car park, hurried up to Brad's apartment, and began to fling off her clothes as soon as the door was closed behind her. Under her gabardine suit she was slicked with sweat—late or not, she needed a shower.

The warm water eased some of the urgency out of her. Ten minutes late, half an hour late—what difference would it make? Better, in any case, to arrive relaxed and looking good, rather than grubby and work-weary.

She threw open a wardrobe and the drawers where she kept her underclothes. Her fingers slithered sensuously over a white silk teddy, edged with pale blue lace, that Brad had bought her the previous weekend. He had treated her to a whole heap of new underclothes, laughing off her protests that it was an extravagance. Sure it was, he agreed, but he liked them! And sure, she looked great without them, but she looked pretty good in them too!

What was more, she felt even better than she looked, she decided, rolling on one sheer stocking, then pausing to glance in the mirrored wardrobe doors that lined one wall of the bedroom. Brad had awakened a side of her personality she had barely known existed—a sexy, playful side. She felt a familiar tightening in her abdomen as she envisaged what would happen when Brad helped her take her clothes off later that evening.

They might have their difficulties, but there were so many marvellous things about their relationship that together they would surely find a way to overcome them.

Rapidly she pulled on a silky sky-blue two-piece, rolled her hair into a quick pleat, fastened gold studs in her ears, and slid a couple of gold bangles up her left arm. That would do. The outfit wasn't elaborate, but it was emphatically a 'boss's fiancée' outfit—chic and sophisticated, with a stylish cut and perfect fit. Brad had helped her choose this, too, in one of the pretty boutiques in Rouen's charming old quarter.

Two minutes to do her make-up, then she grabbed a small clutch-bag, checked that it held keys and tissues and change, and hurried down to the car park.

It was ten to seven when she swung open the heavy doors of the ECF Building, threw a smile over to the porter behind the reception desk, and made her way to the express lift.

She heard the hum of voices from the boardroom as soon as the lift doors opened. Thank goodness, she wasn't too late. She slipped in as unobtrusively as she could, hoping Brad wouldn't register the exact time of her arrival. He was standing at the other side of the room, she saw immediately—she could hardly fail to, when he was the tallest man in the room. But he was facing the door, perhaps even watching out for her, and he rapidly caught her eye.

He couldn't readily disengage himself from the portly moustached man he was talking to, though, so she gave him a wry smile of apology, and glanced around to see who else was there.

It wasn't a huge do. There were maybe two dozen people milling around in the open space before the huge mahogany table—most of them male, although the willowy figure of Juliette was among them. About half of them were familiar to her. She guessed that all but a couple of the ECF employees would leave after the drinks, and that she and Brad, plus Michel Guerard and his wife Laure, a tiny, exquisitely pretty Belgian woman, would be escorting the visitors on to supper.

'Good evening, Mademoiselle Miller.'

'Hello, Monsieur Guerard.' The western area manager was a formal type—not easy company. But just the person Tara needed to see!

'I'm glad you've arrived at last,' Monsieur Guerard continued. 'Can I take you to meet Monsieur Brillac from the Piazza Group?'

'In a minute, but could I have a word with you first?'

'Certainly—what about?'

'The insurance inspection I did today, on your Louviers warehouse.'

'Ah, yes, Jacques Michelet's place. He was helpful, I hope? And you found it an improvement on Montelimar?'

'In many ways, yes, but there's a serious problem with the water supply to the sprinkler system.'

She outlined the situation quickly, mindful that she really ought to circulate before the party broke up, but unwilling to pass up this opportunity to pave the way for getting the fire pump approved.

Guerard frowned when she came to the pump and tank. 'That'll be expensive?'

'I'm afraid it will, but it's very necessary. You see, if the sprinklers don't have adequate water——'

'Tara,' a low voice interrupted, as two hands trapped her by the waist. 'What kept you?'

'I'll tell you later, darling.' She glanced up at Brad, then back to Guerard. 'I guess this isn't the time to discuss it.'

'Later, perhaps. Or if it's going to be very expensive, then it will be a decision for Monsieur Hamilton.'

'What're you talking about, honey?'

'The fire protection at Louviers.'

'I'll see you later,' Guerard said diplomatically. 'Hamilton, you'd like me to stop the waitresses serving wine now?'

'In a couple of minutes,' Brad said curtly. He waited till Guerard had moved off, then said in a fierce whisper, 'For God's sake, I told you six.'

'I just couldn't make it,' Tara said assertively. 'Brad, I'm sorry. Now who should I meet?'

For a moment she thought Brad was going to persist with his complaint, but this wasn't the place, and he knew it. 'Paul Revert,' he said briefly. 'Chief buyer for Piazza.'

'Has he signed the contract?'

'Not yet, so pile on the charm, OK?'

'I sure will.' She was beginning to feel acutely weary after her long day, but she gave him a brilliant smile, and let him lead her across to the plump man he had been talking to earlier.

'You did a great job tonight, honey.' Brad held open the passenger door of his Ferrari till Tara was safely installed, then shut it and strode around to the driver's side. Ignoring his seatbelt, he leaned over and pulled Tara to him with one hand, sliding the other on to her silk-covered thigh.

'I enjoyed it,' Tara said softly. And she had, knowing that she had done a good job of helping Brad by being charming to his clients. 'I'll be glad when we're holidaying in Paris and we can relax more, though.'

'You can relax now.'

'That's what you call this?' she teased. His fingers,

drawing circles with deceptive laziness on the inner skin of her thigh, were having the very opposite effect on her.

'Not exactly,' Brad agreed. His mouth sought out hers, his tongue easing her lips apart and speaking the sensual language of love.

'We'd better get home fast,' Tara murmured.

'I thought we'd stop on the way.'

'Where?'

'I know a place. It's a warm night.'

'Outside?'

'A very beautiful——' his lips touched her temples, the tip of her nose, just brushed her mouth once more '—and very private place.'

'OK,' she whispered back.

He slowly eased away from her, and started the car. Out he drove, into the stream of night-time traffic that flowed along the *quais* bordering the Seine, then branching off on to a road that rose up above the river valley, into the chalk hills that bordered it.

As they swooped around hairpin bends, there were spectacular views down to the valley and the city, with its lights and the dark shapes of its church towers. Brad drove on, off the main road, into a silent, wooded area. He pulled the car off the road, flicked off the head-lights, and got out, walking round to help Tara out as well.

Through the trees, she could just glimpse the lights of the city, but otherwise it was miraculously silent.

'We're high,' she said wonderingly.

'In every sense,' Brad murmured.

His body loomed black against the night shadows, as he drew her to him and kissed her. Then he drew away, returning to the car to fetch a coat which he had left in the back, and then led her through the trees. Within

yards they thinned out, and the view was spread in a
glittering carpet beneath them.

Tara only had a moment to register the glory of the
place, though, before Brad drew her down on to the
coat which he had spread on the ground.

The ground beneath her was hard, but smooth. Brad,
drawing her to him, felt big and warm, dark and
exciting. One arm was around her shoulders; his other
was free, his hand resuming its earlier exploration. He
untucked her silk top from her skirt and slid cool
fingers beneath, rediscovering the curves of her breast.

'Mmm. Silk. . .on silk. . .on silk.'

The silk of her top, the silk of her teddy beneath it,
slithered away from the hidden silk of her breast,
exposing a rosy nipple to his questing fingers. He bent
his head, and replaced them with the searing warmth
of his mouth. Tara gasped. She felt his hands and
mouth register her reaction, and expertly move to
intensify it, sending pulsing waves of pleasure through
her body.

He moved his hand to her thigh, searching out the
band of bare skin above her stocking-tops. His touch
was electric. She trembled with anticipation as his
fingers found the little row of buttons that fastened the
bottom edge of the teddy.

'Like what I'm wearing?' she whispered.

'Mmm. Feels good, but it's not made for the dark.'

All those little buttons—which he steadily unfastened, one-handed. The final one snapped free, and
with a little grunt of triumph he slid his fingers into the
warm, moist crevice above them.

Tara gasped again. 'Darling. . .'

'Touch me,' Brad urged in a low voice, before his
mouth reclaimed hers. His fingers were moving more
and more rapidly, stirring the undercurrent of sexual

excitement she had shared with him all evening into a unstoppable surge.

The dark, the starry cavern of sky above them, the dizzying pattern of light far below, all brought magic to their encounter. Tara felt as if she was suspended in space, conscious of nothing but the mounting frenzy of her response to Brad's touch. Her mind was floating free, but with an effort she brought it back to earth for long enough to focus on his clothing, and dispose of the barriers of cloth and zip.

His maleness throbbed in her hand, telling her that his arousal was as intense as her own. As he moved to position himself above her, she guided him in the dark. Their bodies joined in the ultimate embrace, and with the joining came the first deep tremors of her release.

His hands were under her buttocks now, holding her hard against him as he thrust deeper and deeper. Her body burned, all sensation focused on the hot core that was his possession of her. The tremors intensified into a hot ecstasy that engulfed her.

She felt him swell within her, felt his fingers clench on her, and as her explosion faded she was conscious of his beginning, burgeoning and fading into limp satisfaction.

Her eyes had closed at some point. She opened them not to darkness, but to the magical light of a thousand stars, stencilling the outline of Brad's body against the sky—from the blacker darkness of his eyes, trapping and holding hers, to the engulfing shadow of his body as he bent once more to kiss her—this time with a gentleness that spelled urgency left far behind.

'Better. Much better.'

'True,' she whispered back.

She still felt languorously satisfied after they had returned to the car, and were driving home. Her eyes turned to his strong profile. His eyes were fixed firmly on the road, and he drove with brisk efficiency, as if he had set their lovemaking to the back of his mind already.

What was he thinking of? She wasn't sure. In some ways she didn't yet know him all that well, she thought to herself, she couldn't yet follow his unspoken thoughts. He might want to be close to her, but his deep-seated inhibitions, and the sheer pressure on their time—not to mention the physical passion that overwhelmed them whenever they were alone—had kept them from talking much about their experiences of the past, and hopes for the future.

Could she ask him?

No, no, he was concentrating on driving in the dark, and he wouldn't want to start off on reminiscences now. As for the future, that was a subject fraught with problems still, and she didn't want to provoke an argument at the end of a lovely evening.

She had been lucky to avoid one, she slowly realised, as her mind came back to her late arrival at the boardroom. Perhaps Brad was thinking about that? Well, if he was, it was perhaps as well he wasn't choosing to share his thoughts with her!

CHAPTER EIGHT

'Six thirty. Stir it, honey.'

Tara turned over and groaned. The warm sheets seemed to cocoon her, the duvet moulding itself to her body. Getting out of bed and on the road was the last thing she wanted.

Brad wasn't taking 'umph' for an answer, though. A large hand grabbed the top edge of the duvet and pulled it down.

'Ouch!'

'Don't tell me you're cold, it's a warm morning and the sun's up already. Time to hit the track.'

'Slave-driver! Don't you ever get a hangover?'

'Not on two glasses of wine, and nor do you, so snap to it!'

She relented sufficiently to stretch her limbs and yawn. Bringing her eyes up to Brad as she contracted her muscles again, she was conscious of him looking at her naked body.

And liking what he saw, she guessed. He had proved that over again once they had got back home the evening before, but when two people were as physically compatible as she and Brad, satiation didn't seem to last for long. She would have preferred to get her exercise horizontally, by dragging him back to bed with her.

But he was already dressed in brief running-shorts and singlet, and looking revoltingly wide awake. She lay there for a moment, drinking in the sight of him. Funny, she thought, how brief garments often looked more sexy than nothing at all. Just the sight of those muscular thighs sprinkled with dark hair, of the thicker hair that curled around the scooped neck of his singlet, of the biceps that flexed as he leaned down to take her hand and pull on it, was enough to send her weak with memories and longings.

He wouldn't stay in such superb shape, though, if he didn't have the discipline to run at six-thirty every morning! She, too, liked the feeling of jogging along next to him, and of arriving at work feeling her body was well honed and her mind ready for anything. Right now she might be stumbling to the bathroom and groping for her toothbrush, but in an hour she would feel clean and glowing and bright-eyed.

Brad was warming up in the living area when she emerged from the bathroom, clad in an outfit almost as brief as his. Tara just had time for a couple of dozen arm-swings and straight-arm push-ups, then he was urging her out of the door.

The sky was still faintly golden near the horizon, the day's quiet broken by little more than bird-song. Moving silently in their running-shoes, they slid into a steady medium pace as they struck out through the village and down to the riverbank. The heady smell of fresh bread greeted them as they passed the little bakery. Tara's breath began to come hard but evenly, and she stretched out her strides to try to keep up with Brad's longer legs and greater strength.

Keeping to a pace that was comfortable for her wouldn't have exercised him fully, though, and when they came to a point where the riverside track forked he glanced round with a grin, as usual, then headed off on the upward track. He would edge round a couple of cornfields, then join her again at some point as she was urging her weary feet up the hill through the village and back to the apartment.

When she had started running with him, he had caught up with her every morning at the very foot of the village hill, but even in three weeks she had grown leaner and fitter, and today she was paying for their *gros pain* and *brioches* when he reached the door of the bakery. He was breathing almost as hard as she had been, and he reached out and touched her arm with a smile, acknowledging her improvement.

'And I thought I was fit before,' she murmured, as they dropped to a rapid walk for the last stretch home.

'You were. You're just fitter now.'

'True.' She smiled to herself. She had felt twice as full of energy and enthusiasm, ten times as aware of her own body, since she had been with Brad—and she guessed that only a tiny part of that was thanks to their morning runs.

'It'll be an easy day for me today,' she went on thoughtfully. 'There's nothing much to checking out an office block. The sprinkler layout's regular, there are complete plans of the block which I only need to trace, and I can even walk up proper stairs all the way to the roof.'

'You have to go on the roof?'

'Oh, always! I never know what I'll find up there, either.'

'And you're lunching with me—at one, say?'

'Should suit me fine. With luck I'll be finished by then.'

'Good timing,' Brad assured her. It was Friday, the last day before her vacation. She would have the afternoon to write up her reports, and then with luck she would be able to post them on Saturday morning, and forget all about work for two whole weeks.

Brad fumbled for the key he kept in his waist-belt,
let them into the apartment, and after dropping the
bread and *brioches* in the kitchen they made straight
for the shower. It was a ritual for them to share it—
and it was the best part of the day, Tara sometimes
thought. She loved feeling super-charged and virtuous
after the demanding exercise, and yet enjoying the
erotic pleasure of soaping and caressing Brad's strong
body.

He shaved, she slicked on a little light make-up and
fastened back her hair, and they dressed quickly. Then
they shared the small chores of making fresh coffee,
squeezing orange juice, and carrying bread and
brioches, butter, apricot jam, and the rest of their
breakfast equipment out to the table on the terrace
overlooking the river.

Tara's eyes shifted from the coffee-pot, to the stun-
ning view of sunlight sparkling on the sinuous curve of
the Seine, to Brad, city-suited now, shoes shiny-black,
hair still slick with damp from the shower.

'Darling,' she said slowly, 'I hate to be tedious, but
can we talk about the fire protection at Louviers?'

Brad's eyes rose slowly to hers, and she saw his
heavy brows lower over them.

'Can we *what*?'

'I know it's hardly breakfast-table conversation, but
it's important. I'll only have today to persuade Michel
Guerard to approve the fire pump, and I want to be
able to tell him I've got your backing.'

'Is this what you were talking to him about last
night?'

'That's right. You see, there's a sprinkler system at
the warehouse, but——'

'Just a minute,' Brad interrupted. 'I wasn't saying
anything in front of Guerard, but now you've brought

it up, let's get this clear. It was bad enough you turning up an hour late when I'd told you I needed you there— but what the hell did you think you were doing, grabbing one of my senior staff at a reception for clients, and starting in on *fire pumps*?'

'It was only for five minutes!' Tara protested. 'And it's important, Brad. There are some major problems at Louviers, and it's got to be my priority to see them put right.'

'Your priority!'

'Yes! It's my job, Brad. Of course I take it seriously.'

'But Tara, for God's sake! Your priority! Maybe I'm being dumb, but I was reckoning your *priority* was supporting me!'

'But it's for your benefit too,' Tara pointed out. 'It's your warehouse I'm talking about, and at the moment it's grossly under-protected.'

'So what?' Brad leaned forward, large hands grabbing the sides of the small wooden table. 'Tara, you're my fiancée, and soon you're going to be my wife. That's your life, that's your future, that's what *matters*, not this damn job that you're about to throw up anyway. I asked you to come along last night to *support me*. Those are important clients. You're supposed to work on them, for heaven's sake. You're supposed to charm them, to help me impress them. So what do I find? You're so wrapped up in your sprinkler systems that you don't even turn up till I'm about to give you up for lost, and then instead of making up for lost time you grab my western region manager and start talking about fire pumps!'

'All right, so I did! But Brad, you don't seem to understand! This is a vital issue. It's critically import-ant! Without proper fire protection that warehouse could burn to the ground tomorrow, and then where would your clients be?'

'Will it hell!' Brad's whole body was rigid with anger. He rose to his feet, slowly, deliberately, and stood towering over her.

'That warehouse,' he said in a cold voice, 'has stood there for ten years or more, and you can't persuade me it's suddenly turned into a powder keg overnight. And you tell me that's the most vital issue facing me? Are you crazy? Don't you have *any idea* what it's like to run a company like ECF?'

'All right,' she said nervously, 'maybe I exaggerated a little—but only a little, Brad. I did think it was important; I still do. I know your clients are important, too, but I don't believe I really offended them.'

'You offended me.'

'Darling, I'm sorry.' She scrambled to her feet, and moved to put her arms round him. 'Honestly, I didn't mean to. Of course you're more important to me than Insco is, a million times more important. It's just that— well, sometimes I get the feeling that ECF's more important to *you*, than I am.'

'That's not so,' Brad said levelly.

'I hope not. You see, darling, the way I see it is: there's us, you and me, and our first priority is to find a lifestyle where we can be together, and both be happy and fulfilled. But I sometimes think the way *you* see it is: there's this monolith called ECF. You want us to be together, but your starting point isn't us, and how we can be happy—it's ECF.'

'Be reasonable, Tara.'

'I am being! But don't you see? At the moment I've got a job I like, and so have you. All right, we can't easily combine the two jobs and still be happy together, so something's got to give. Most likely my job's got to go, and I understand that, and accept it. But once it's gone, I've got to find a new lifestyle that will fulfil me, and at the moment I can't see how I'm going to do that.'

'Tara, you're making problems where there aren't any. I've told you, there'll be plenty for you to do when we're——'

'What?' she fiercely interrupted. 'What *am* I supposed to do? Paint my nails and do my hair all day, and come out in the evenings to chat up your clients? Is that what you honestly imagine I'll do? Because I won't, Brad! All right, my job isn't as high-powered as yours, but it's interesting and fulfilling, and it's been my life for longer than you've worked for ECF—nearly as long as you've worked for SHP. And you want me to give it up so I can be a part-time hostess for you! Be fair! Be reasonable!'

'Now you be fair!' Brad growled back. 'Your job and mine aren't the same, and it's no good pretending they are. You can leave Insco—you could leave it tomorrow. I can't leave SHP. That's fixed, and if you want to marry me you'd better get used to the idea.'

'It doesn't have to be!'

'Oh, yes, it does!'

'Why? It's just a job, Brad! Just an ordinary job! OK, it pays you lots of money and gives you lots of power and does wonders for your ego, but it's only a job! And sometimes, when I think of what you've given up already for it. . .'

'Now just a minute.' His hands gripped her shoulders and tightened, moving her a short distance away from him so that he could stare down into her face. 'Don't let's confuse issues,' he said icily. 'All right, I gave up plenty for SHP, my painting included, although that wasn't the loss you seem to be kidding yourself it was.

It wasn't an easy decision even so, but I told you, I hadn't any choice then, and I don't have any choice now. I don't even want any choice. SHP's my family firm. It was my grandfather's life and my father's life, and now it's my life, and that's the way it's going to stay. And if you're going to marry me you'll just have to fit in with it, because I'm going to keep on working for it for the next thirty years at least.'

'But SHP isn't your family firm!'

'I told you it was.'

'You didn't! All right, you told me you gave up your painting for the family firm, but——'

'So?' Brad asked grimly.

Tara stared back at him, wildly. Then the dreadful certainty behind his hard gaze sunk into her, and she went limp in his hands. 'Oh, no,' she whispered.

'Oh yes. SHP: Simon Hamilton Plastics.'

'I never. . .'

'Smile,' Brad said coldly. 'You're marrying the heir to one of the world's largest corporations.' His hands gripped tighter. '*Or are you?*'

Was she? At that moment, she honestly didn't know. She didn't know anything, beyond the fierce painful grip of Brad's hands, and the whirling of her own head.

Brad's grip lasted only a second longer, though, before he abruptly released her, turning immediately and striding back into the apartment.

She fell back on to her chair, and let her head fall into her hands. She was still sitting there when Brad reappeared, jingling his car keys in his hand.

'It's past eight,' he said tersely. 'Get moving.'

No! her head screamed. She didn't want to move, especially with him. She wanted to retreat inside herself, to hug her hurt and confusion, to have time to come to terms with all he'd said.

But her car was back in ECF's car park, Michel Guerard was waiting to discuss her inspection, and Brad was standing there waiting too, tall and forbidding. She couldn't opt out—pride wouldn't let her. Slowly, she got to her feet, pushed past him into the living area, and gathered together her papers.

'I'm ready,' she said dully.

'Then let's go.'

They didn't speak as they walked down to the car park, and got into the Ferrari. In silence, Brad started the car and swung out on to the main road. The morning sun flashed on the windscreen.

'You knew I didn't know,' Tara said bleakly.

'I wasn't sure.'

'Why didn't you tell me—tell me properly?'

He didn't answer immediately, and she turned her head painfully to look at him.

Brad Hamilton. One tall, good-looking American male whom, it seemed, she didn't know at all.

He shrugged. 'I guess I was just following my usual policy,' he said flatly. 'At first, anyway.'

'You mean you don't tell anyone?'

'Uh-huh. For all the obvious reasons.'

'Which are?'

'It changes the way people see me—people at work, especially.'

Yes, yes, it would. He was young for his job; but not knowing, people would think as she had thought—that it was exceptional merit that had carried him so far, so fast. But if they saw the rest—the years spent as a painter, the relatives on the Board—what would they think, then?

What did she think, come to that? Right now, nothing. She was too close to him, and she couldn't pretend that she had the ability to stand back and re-evaluate all she had learned in an instant.

'Oh, well,' she said wryly. 'At least I didn't love you for your money.'

'That helped.' If he noticed the past tense, he didn't mention it.

They didn't speak again until the Ferrari drew up in the underground car park. Brad parked, with controlled precision, in the empty space next to Tara's hired Peugeot. He got out of the car immediately, and Tara followed suit.

'I'll see you lunchtime,' he said. Then he strode off towards the private lift, gesturing briefly to the adjoining door. 'You take that one. Guerard's on the twelfth floor.'

A morning's work gave Tara no more time for thought about her situation; every moment was taken up with her inspection of the headquarters building. Although there were no unexpected problems, there were water supplies to test, fire extinguishers to check, calculations to make—and finally, a wearing interview with Michel Guerard.

At least she had paved the way the night before for discussing the fire pump needed at Louviers, even if the personal cost had been greater than she had expected. It didn't help much, though. Monsieur Guerard seemed no more understanding than Jacques Michelet had been. That warehouse had a full sprinkler system, he pointed out, and no way did it figure in the queue for further expenditure on fire protection.

He simply didn't understand that sprinklers were useless without sufficient water to supply them, Tara thought irritably, after a fruitless half-hour attempt to explain Insco's position to him. Security was only one of his many responsibilities, and like so many managers he didn't know enough about the subject to fully appreciate her arguments.

What ECF didn't have was a corporate security manager, fully trained in fire protection, as well as in other aspects of security work. And how they needed one! Such people weren't easy to find, however. Only a very few companies trained fire protection engineers to Insco's standards, and. . .

And, she went on to herself with dawning excitement, many Insco-insured corporations took advantage of that fact, by hiring ex-Insco staff to act as their security managers. The job was more desk-bound than factory inspecting, and Insco inspectors often made the sideways move when they were looking to settle down.

And she had thought there wasn't a job for her in Rouen! Couldn't this be her job? Wouldn't it solve all their problems?

The more she thought about it, the more perfect a solution it seemed. What better way would there be to give Brad her support, than to work for SHP itself? What better way to make her working life mesh with his?

Her spirits seemed to rise as fast as the private lift, as she made her way to the top floor to join him for lunch. Only this morning everything had looked so hopeless, and now it seemed that it had all fallen into place.

The lift purred to a rapid halt, and she stepped out. Juliette glanced up from behind her desk, but for once Tara felt no irritation at seeing the blonde Frenchwoman who worked so closely with Brad. If he appointed her security manager, *she* would be working closely with him, too!

'Darling,' she announced, as she pushed open the door to his office, 'I've had a wonderful idea!'

'Is it lunchtime already?' Brad enquired, glancing up from his telephone and notepad with a harassed expression.

'It's ten past one, so I'm late, actually.'

'Damn!'

How friendly! There wasn't a smile to soften the words, either. Still, he hadn't been given any reason to set their quarrel behind him yet, so she had to make allowances.

'It's all right, I'll wait here till you're ready.'

'Here' was a conversation area in the corner of his big office, with spikily-formal chairs arranged around a low table spread with magazines. Since Brad hadn't answered, instead turning back to his telephone, Tara drifted over to it, sat in the nearest chair, and picked up a copy of the London *Financial Times*.

She read the front and back pages, and still Brad was absorbed on the telephone. Every few seconds she glanced across at him. He didn't look her way at all.

Busy, busy. Of course he was. She knew that; he hadn't really needed to point out that obvious fact that morning.

She had thought, though, that SHP was. . . Well, it was no good fretting about that. Brad clearly didn't have any choice about working for his family firm, now or in the future.

No, the choices were hers; they always had been. Somehow she had to make him understand that his being over-busy wasn't a reason for her to become *less* busy. If she spent her life hanging around waiting for him to finish work, she would go crazy. What she needed was a job that could complement his!

'Just one more call,' Brad called over, in a louder

voice. With a half-smile, Tara set her briefcase on the
magazine table and opened it. Decorative wives might
get bored in these situations; fire protection experts
had work of their own to do.

Not much of it, actually, but at least she could make
some additional notes for her report, and draft an
introductory paragraph or two. She jotted down a
series of comments, flicked over the page on her
shorthand pad, then glanced up to find that Brad had
replaced his telephone, and was standing over her.

'I can spare half an hour,' he said challengingly.

'So can I.' She stood up, sweeping her papers back
into her briefcase, and smiled at him.

This smile wasn't returned either, and the happy
optimism with which she'd come to his office began to
fade a little. He didn't have to be quite so distant and
aggressive! All right, they had had a row, but she at
least was motivated to find a solution to their differences, and he might have shown the same inclination.

Walking so rapidly that Tara had to trot to keep up,
Brad led the way to a chrome and glass self-service
restaurant a few blocks away. It was a typically French
place, serving fast food, but with gourmet overtones.
They picked out a lobster mayonnaise and salad each
from the temptingly arranged display, and found a
corner table.

'Brad,' Tara began, 'let me tell you my idea.'

She outlined it swiftly, wanting to clear the air
between them as soon as possible. Obviously the details
would have to be worked out, but if he could just agree
in principle. . .

There was silence when she finished.

'Don't you think it's the ideal solution?' she pressed.

'Let me get this clear,' Brad said tersely. 'I'm to
create a job for you. Paid, presumably. . .'

'Obviously!'

'. . .so that you can do what?'

'So I can co-ordinate security arrangements—and perhaps insurance arrangements too, with some help from the Accounts Department.'

'So you can carry on working.'

'That's right.'

'But I don't want you to carry on working.'

'I need to work, Brad. It isn't the money, it's me, and what I do with myself. That job needs doing, and I need to do it.'

'It's never needed doing before.'

'And look at the result! Look at Louviers, for instance, where a huge amount of money has been spent on a sprinkler system that's worse than useless! You'll have to get that put right, and somebody—and not Jacques Michelet!—will have to supervise the installation of the fire pump, and——'

'There won't be a fire pump.'

'Brad, there has to be. It's not an optional extra, it's an essential part of your fire precautions. It simply has to be done.'

She met his eyes, to underline her conviction, only to shy away, though, in sheer confusion. He was looking at her oddly, with what she might almost have taken for hatred.

'You're obsessed,' he said, in a strange cold voice.

'Of course I'm not obsessed! I'm worried, and rightly worried, because it's a dangerous situation there. But I'm not obsessed, Brad!'

'Oh, yes, you are,' he went on. 'All you ever think about is sprinkler systems. I told you I've other problems. I've a budget that's already stretched to breaking point. I've factories like Montelimar, so badly run I barely know how to start to turn them round. I've a

Main Board in Boston on my back, nagging at me to up the profits and justify taking over ECF. I've told you I need a wife who'll give me a hundred per cent support. I come to you for a moment's respite, and what do I get? Demands that I spend money I haven't got on a fire pump that isn't needed! You're crazy, Tara, crazy.'

'Brad, you're the crazy one, if you react like this! It's not just a question of a job for me—even though I thought you'd like the idea! I thought it would solve all our problems!—but it's the warehouse, too. It's ECF, Brad, and the protection they need!'

'Well they can't have it, and you can't have it. If you marry me I'm not having you working, Tara. I'm not sharing you with a load of sprinkler systems.'

'Brad, please——'

Brad was already shoving his half-eaten lunch to one side, though, and getting to his feet.

'You can't have marriage to me and a job, Tara,' he said sharply. 'So you'd better decide which you want, and fast.'

He didn't wait for an answer, throwing a banknote down on to the table, and leaving her alone in the restaurant.

He meant it, she thought numbly, as she retraced her steps to ECF and her car. He had to mean it. He hadn't even listened properly to her suggestion.

And that surely meant that it was SHP that was his priority, not her. He didn't really care about making her happy; all he cared about was getting 'support' so that he could throw himself even more whole-heartedly into running the European operation.

Tara loved Brad, and she wanted to find a way forward for them. She hated to see him like this; she

wanted to make *him* happy. But how could she make
him happy by becoming unhappy herself? Little as she
wanted great riches, she was prepared to come to terms
with Brad's position in life—but she couldn't be contented in the kind of life he envisaged for her, and she
knew it.

And he accused her of being obsessed! It was he who
was really obsessed, with SHP and all that it stood for.
What she couldn't live with was the knowledge that he
was putting the company first, and her second.

Unless he compromised, unless he revised that order,
then she couldn't possibly marry him.

Would he? Could he? Everything had happened so
fast. A day before they had been on the best of terms,
she hadn't known he was the heir to SHP, and he
hadn't given her his ultimatum.

She herself had barely had time to take in that
morning's revelations. Brad, working flat out, must
have had even less time to consider the position. He
might well have expected that she would give in, if he
pushed her. Surely he didn't really want them to
separate over the issue of her job!

She didn't, that was for sure—but she couldn't accept
him on his terms, either. At least, right now she felt
she couldn't, but she didn't want to come to too quick
a decision.

She had two more weeks to spend in France, two
precious weeks of holiday time. Surely it was worth
spending that time with Brad, talking to him, trying to
persuade him? Then, if they still couldn't agree, she
would have no choice but to admit that she wasn't the
woman for him.

But she *was* the woman for him, her body and soul
cried out to her. She loved him, and she belonged with

him. Why, why wouldn't he help to make that possible for her?

She reached her car, got in, and sat there for several minutes, her heart and mind too full for her to think of driving off. Another car swept into the car park, and, embarrassed at being caught sitting there by the driver, she fumbled for the ignition key and started the car.

She drove fast, angrily, back to Brad's apartment, stormed in, and threw her briefcase down on one of the designer sofas. Bloody designers, bloody huge corporations, bloody money. SHP was huge, *huge*, one of the biggest privately-owned corporations in the world. Brad must have billions. And what did it bring him? Not the freedom to do as he wanted with his life, not the carefree happiness he'd surely known years before, but this tense, pressurised, *miserable* lifestyle that he expected her to share! Well, she wasn't doing it! She wasn't going to live in the prison he'd made of his life. If he wanted to marry her, he'd have to put their relationship first!

The telephone buzzed. Brad, presumably—nobody else would expect anyone to be there. Phoning to say what? Nothing constructive, she was willing to bet!

She picked up the receiver and slammed it down again, then went into the kitchen to put on the kettle. She wanted coffee—hot, strong coffee.

The phone rang again.

Curse him. He could have guessed from the first attempt what mood she was in. So why try again?

Was it possible. . .?

She let it ring six times, then snatched up the receiver.

'*Allo*? Mademoiselle Miller?'

It wasn't Brad's voice after all, but a strange French male voice. 'Yes,' she said tentatively.

'It's Michelet. From Louviers. You remember.'

'Of course I remember, Monsieur Michelet.'

'You must come. Come now. Hurry! The warehouse is on fire!'

CHAPTER NINE

TARA first saw the plume of black smoke when she was more than a mile off. The fire must have taken firm hold before Michelet had phoned her, and it had taken her some time to get through to Jim Backley in London, to leave a message with Juliette, and to start the Peugeot with fumbling fingers.

As she neared the outskirts of Louviers, she saw the shimmering heat haze that hung over the site. The first black specks began to drift on to the car windscreen, and a familiar mixture of horror and exhilaration took hold of her. She had seen only a handful of really large fires, but every one affected her in the same way.

A fire like this, a huge blaze, drove everything else out of your mind. She had barely thought about Brad since Michelet had rung.

The main road that passed the industrial estate was blocked by a police cordon several hundred yards from the warehouse. She parked her car on the roadside, and showed her business card to the police. With it as authorisation they let her pass, and as she neared the warehouse the air became thick with the pungent smell of plastic burning.

Plastics—one of the worst of all materials to catch fire. The poisonous fumes made fires like this especially dangerous for the fire-fighters, and they were murder to extinguish. This one would rage now until the warehouse was completely destroyed. A section of the flimsy roof had gone already, and the flames were leaping high against the empty blue sky.

Several fire-engines were already in service, with emergency water supplies and high-pressure hoses, but the narrow arcs of water looked pitifully inadequate when set against the inferno.

The only way to beat fires like this was to catch them quickly. That was why Insco insisted that automatic sprinklers be installed in warehouses. Whenever and wherever a fire started, the sprinkler valve overhead shattered quickly, directing a powerful spray of water exactly where it was needed.

With highly combustible items like plastic packaged in cardboard, the fire would spread fast, though, and the heat rapidly build up to trigger perhaps ten sprinklers. Unless the water supply was really powerful, instead of a downpour there would be a bare trickle coming from each one; and the fire wouldn't be fully extinguished, but would rage on to trigger more sprinklers, spread that inadequate water still more widely. . .and this was the result.

A textbook example, Tara thought sadly, gazing on the devastation in progress before her eyes.

Fortunately, the ECF warehouse was well separated from the other units on the small industrial estate, and most of the firemen's efforts were now devoted to saturating the neighbouring buildings, stopping sparks and flaming debris from spreading the fire still further.

There really wasn't anything she could do, except mourn. Nobody could get inside what remained of the warehouse now; even from where she paused near the estate entrance, she was being battered by the intense heat. With all her skill, she wouldn't be able to improve on the job the firefighters were doing. She had had to come, but all she could do was to join the small audience of workmen.

She took a side path between two other warehouses,

trying to edge closer without being suffocated by the heat and the vile smell. At the end of the path a small knot of men were standing, and among them she made out the familiar figure of Jacques Michelet.

'Mademoiselle Miller.' Michelet's face was streaked in black, his shoulders drooped, and his expression was haunted. His jaws worked inexhaustibly, as if his chewing-gum was the only thing keeping him sane. 'You think us every kind of fool, *non*?'

'I doubt it's your fault; it happens so easily. What started it?'

'How am I to know? How is anyone to tell? One moment all was fine, then the next moment Gilles here turned round and saw flames in a corner of the warehouse. He grabbed the extinguisher, but——'

'But that'd be useless if the boxes had caught,' Tara completed. 'At least everyone's out safely, I hope?'

Michelet nodded. As Tara knew, the warehouse had only three staff; most of the people standing around had come from the adjoining industrial units.

'And the sprinklers went off all right?'

'Yes, but so fast,' Gilles, a tall, cadaverous man, put in. 'I think, cardboard, it burns slow, *non*? But the flames here, they go whoosh in seconds, like somebody throwing paraffin on a bonfire. And the sprinklers, they go pfft—one, then another, then five or six, or more. So quick. You see, they soak me before I run for the door.'

Actually Gilles didn't look wet to Tara, but his overalls had probably dried almost immediately in this infernal heat. All of the watchers were rapidly being covered in flaking debris, and they had to shout to make themselves heard over the roar of the flames.

'Come back a little,' she yelled.

'But I think we must. . .'

She nodded; she understood only too well how Jacques Michelet must wish he could do something—anything. 'But you cannot,' she cried. 'Come right back. I want to know more.'

Michelet hesitated, then he and Gilles peeled away from the other men, nodding curtly to them, and followed Tara back to a chain-link fence that marked the edge of the estate.

'A whoosh, you said?' she asked earnestly. 'You're sure of that?'

'Yes, yes. I couldn't mistake that. A. . .whoosh, that's the only word for it.'

'And did you smell anything?'

'In this?' Gilles wrinkled his nose.

'Before the plastic began to burn. At first, when you saw the cardboard catch fire, when you heard that whoosh. Did you. . .?'

'Smell what? What kind of thing?'

Paraffin of course, you idiot, Tara wanted to shout. Did you smell paraffin, or petrol, or anything else that might be used to light a fire? But she couldn't put words into Gilles' mouth, not when he'd already mentioned paraffin himself.

She shrugged. 'I don't know—anything.' It probably hadn't started like that, anyway. A stray match or electrical spark could easily have triggered the fire. Gilles might have imagined his whoosh. Maybe the boxes had been smouldering for a while, then the cardboard had suddenly flared up, and that was what he'd been startled by.

'You think. . .arson?' Michelet asked, in a low voice.

'I don't think anything yet,' Tara soberly replied. 'And it's not my job to investigate the cause of the fire—Insco will send over a trained loss-adjuster to do that. But if there's anything you can tell me, it will help. Anything strange you've seen, or heard, or smelled. . .'

'Then your insurance company can turn round and claim it's not their baby,' Michelet said sourly.

'No, that's not it at all. Arson is covered by your policy, but of course we need to know what happened—and so will the police, if there are any suspicious circumstances.'

Michelet turned to Gilles, and Tara felt a flicker of excitement; she was sure some kind of silent message was passing between the two men. They had seen something; they did know something.

'Monsieur Michelet?'

Curse it! An eager young reporter was waving his press card at them. They wouldn't tell her now.

She was so sure of it that she didn't even stop to listen to the reporter interviewing Michelet. Anyway, she wanted to be alone—alone with the fire.

Slipping away from the men, she began to circle round the flaming warehouse, leaving the estate paths to pace through the long, rough grass, keeping just out of danger range.

What a waste. What a stupid, pointless waste. What an irony, when she had formulated her recommendations only the day before.

The day before seemed a long time ago. Even her run that morning seemed a long time ago. So much had happened since, and all of it bad.

She kicked out at the grass in sadness and frustration.

Klunk. Her foot connected with a can hidden in the grass, accidentally kicking it into the air.

Rubbish. Trash, more evidence of human incompetence and stupidity. Surely nobody normally came this way, but even here she had to run across a. . .

A paraffin can.

A paraffin can! She stopped in her tracks, searching the grass for where it had landed. It was only a yard off.

A small can, the two-litre size, she discovered, as she bent down to pick it up. No rust on it, in spite of the rainfall a couple of days earlier. She bent her nose to it, and over the pervading stench of the smoke she caught the pungent fresh whiff of blue paraffin.

Whoosh. Gilles was right, more right than he had known. That was how it must have begun.

But who? Why?

How was she to know? All sorts of people committed arson, for every reason, and no reason at all. This couldn't have been a well-planned crime, or the arsonist wouldn't have left the evidence behind him. It might have been a delinquent schoolboy, a discharged mental patient, an ex-employee with a sky-high grudge against ECF. Maybe whoever it was had even half-wanted to be found out.

If he'd been careless, if he'd just tossed the can away, he might have been careless in other ways, too. There could be fingerprints on the shiny metal. She shouldn't be holding it, except carefully, using a handkerchief or tissue, or even a piece of paper.

Unfortunately, she had none of those things with her. She had taken her suit jacket off in the car, and hadn't brought her briefcase. She glanced down helplessly at her soot-spattered white silk blouse and grey skirt.

Oh well, it was a widely-flared skirt, and fit only for the cleaners already. She spread the thick cotton twill over the can and grasped the wide mental handle through the material. Holding it in this awkward fashion, banging against her knee, she began to hobble back between the remaining warehouses.

Creak. Crash! Swinging round to the noise, she was just in time to see one wall of the warehouse giving way, the steel frame buckling in the heat, and the heavy inset panels falling to the ground.

'Tara!'

At first she hardly took in the shout, wrapped up as she was in the horrifying but enthralling drama unfolding in front of her. Then it was repeated, louder, and in a very familiar voice.

'Brad!' She swung round to face him, dropping the paraffin can that was hampering her movements. Brad here! Her first instinctive reaction was sheer relief at seeing him.

'Tara!' he shouted again, covering the last few strides that separated them, and grabbing her hands. 'You shouldn't be here. It's dangerous. If the fire spread, if anything happened——'

'It won't, darling. We're out of range, and it's under control now, even if it doesn't look it.'

'You're too close. Come away, I won't have you so close.' A towering, flaming heap of wooden pallets and boxes began to list over, and as they fell Brad pulled her against him, shielding her from the heat.

For a moment Tara simply stood there, trembling. She felt a wave of heat lick past them. They really were out of the danger zone, but fear flickered through her body, regardless.

Fear—and a growing awareness of the firm warm body that stood between her and the flames.

It was Brad who moved, taking her arm and urging her away from the burning warehouse.

'Tara, it's dangerous. You shouldn't have come.'

'Of course I should!' she retorted, rather sharply. Now she recognised the instinctive feminine way she was reacting to his protectiveness, and she hated it.

Now she was remembering their earlier quarrel, remembering how impossible it was, and her response to him frightened her.

It wouldn't do to depend on him. He wasn't her protector, he was her gaoler. She hadn't really been in danger, and she knew it, and resented his acting as if she couldn't look after herself.

'It's my job,' she went on, in a harder voice.

'Damn your job! Let's get out of here.'

'But I——' she cut herself short. This wasn't the place to quarrel. He was right, this wasn't the place to be at all. She had learned what she came to learn, and now it really would make sense to get away. 'All right,' she went on, in a taut but sullen voice, 'I'm coming.'

Clunk. Brad's foot hit something. The can! Heavens, for a moment she'd completely forgotten it!

'Just a minute!' she shouted, pulling her arm free of his hand. 'I've got to take——'

'What?' Instinctively, protectively, Brad held her back from bending down to it. He glanced down himself, saw it, and reached out a long arm.

'Don't touch it!'

'Why? What?' His face, reddened by the heat, blackened by soot and smoke, creased into a frown as he froze, and stared at the can.

'There might be fingerprints. We'll have to hand it over to the——'

'Paraffin,' Brad said, in a bewildered voice. 'Paraffin!' He turned puzzled eyes on her. 'Good God, so that's what you were doing here!'

'Obviously it is. Of course I'd look to——'

'My God! You're admitting it?'

Brad had jumped to his feet, and his hands trapped her shoulders, clamping tightly round them. He shook her, dragging her upwards so her feet barely touched the ground.

'Brad, please!'

'Sweet Jesus! I said you were obsessed, but I never imagined for a second you'd——'

'I'd what?'

'No wonder you jumped when I found you! Forgot the evidence, did you? Had to come back to——'

'Brad!' Tara reached out hands that had suddenly found new strength, and pushed at the hard wall of his chest. His fingers tightened on her shoulders, hurting her, but she pushed all the harder, till suddenly he released her and she fell back, panting.

'Oh, lord,' Brad said, in a broken voice, 'I wouldn't have believed it.'

'You can't believe that!'

'Destroying it,' he went on, brokenly. 'Destroying SHP. You know what it means to me. You know it's my life, it's everything I work for, it's. . . And you thought you could get me that way! Oh, no! Burn down every plant in Europe, and I'd never pick a treacherous woman over my work!'

'Brad, you're insane!'

'It's you who's insane. God! I thought I'd learned my lesson after Adrienne, but you're a thousand times worse than she ever was!'

'Brad, I didn't! I couldn't have! You can't really believe it!'

'Get out of my sight!'

She caught at his arm, pleadingly, but he shook her off as if she was an irritating wasp. 'Get lost, now, before I call the police!'

Raw with horror, she stared at him. He couldn't really believe it. There had to be proof, alibis, finger-prints, that would show him. . .

He turned his back on her, bent and picked up the can—carelessly, with his bare hands. Then, without looking round, he strode off down the path between the warehouses.

Tara stood there for a long time, numb, watching him, as the flames crackled, and the ominous plume of black smoke rose up into the air behind her. He disappeared behind a warehouse, but she still stood gazing in the direction he had taken.

'*Mademoiselle.*'

It was no surprise, it brought her no feeling but a kind of weary horror, to glance round and see a *gendarme* touching her arm. She should have left when Brad told her to, she supposed. He'd told them now; he'd accused her. She might go to gaol, at least for a night. And what was that to her, now she had lost Brad for ever?

'*Mademoiselle*, you should not be here,' the *gendarme* said with polite insistence. 'It's dangerous; this is no place for a woman.'

'It's all right. I'll come with you.'

'With me? But I have to stay, *mademoiselle.*'

'Oh.' He wasn't there to arrest her, after all. He wanted to protect her. What a sick irony—she'd had enough for several lifetimes of men who thought they were giving her protection.

'Go, please, *mademoiselle.*'

'It's all right,' Tara said dully. 'I'm going.'

'Well, well. Tara Miller returns.'

'Don't say it like that, Jim. It's the day after my holiday, isn't it?'

'Where've you been?'

'Away.'

'Kiddo,' Jim Backley said, sitting back in his swivelling chair, 'do you have any idea how many people have been looking for you?'

Tara shrugged.

'Sit down,' Jim barked.

She sat.

'You deserve to be fired for pulling that stunt,' Jim said slowly.

'I didn't do it, Jim.'

'Didn't do what?'

'The warehouse; the fire. I can prove it. I've an alibi; I can prove I was still in Rouen when it started.'

'Now just a minute,' Jim interrupted. 'Am I to take it you haven't the slightest idea what's been going on?'

Blanching, she didn't reply.

'You look as if you haven't slept for a fortnight,' Jim said critically. 'You've lost weight, too. Did you really take a holiday?'

'Sort of.' That wasn't precisely the word for the two weeks she had spent driving, walking, thinking, running away—but she wouldn't have confided her state of mind to Jim.

'Oh, well,' he went on, 'let's update you. It was arson at Louviers, of course. They arrested a guy a couple of days after the fire.'

'Who?' Tara asked automatically.

'I forget the name—it's in the file. Some guy Hamilton fired a couple of months ago.'

'Fillol?'

'Yep, that's it. Know him?'

She nodded, numbly.

'The story's in the file. A grudge job—I guess you know more than I do of what was behind it. Apparently the arsonist had an old colleague working at Louviers, and he called in on the guy by chance, the evening after your inspection, on the way back home after an interview for a job he didn't get. Must have seemed like the perfect opportunity to hit back at you and Hamilton in one. He even tried to turn off the water to the sprinklers—reckoned that'd be blamed on you—but the damn fool picked the wrong valve to shut off.'

'Oh.'

'Oh,' Jim echoed. 'That all you've got to say?'

'I'm sorry.'

'For what? Making an enemy?'

'I don't know, Jim, I don't know—for going. I know I should have stayed around, but I—I couldn't.'

'Hamilton?'

She nodded.

'Well, Tara, I don't know what you were thinking, but I do know nobody ever suggested you did it.'

'I guess not.' Slowly, she got to her feet.

'Hamilton's been phoning me every day. He wants to know where you are.'

'Jim, do me a favour? Tell him I don't want to speak to him.'

'How's about *you* do *me* a favour, Tara? You owe me one, remember? For giving you the work in France?'

'Yes, but——'

'Phone him.'

'No. I'll do you a favour, but not that one. Please, Jim.'

'He's a client. A big influential client. The loss has hit ECF hard, but the word from the marketing guys is that Hamilton'll pull it through. He's good, Tara. He's been in that job, what?—six months, and already he's turned around a failing enterprise. He's powerful now, and he'll be more powerful still before he's through. He's not the man to make an enemy of.'

'I'm sorry.'

'So am I, if you're taking that attitude.'

She got to her feet, then paused, not really expecting Jim to let her go.

'Yep, go,' he said brusquely. 'Get a coffee, do some work, get a good night's sleep tonight. I'll talk to you again later.'

'Construction—walls: steel frame with asbestos-cement panels. Floor: concrete. Roof: corrugated asbestos on steel frame. Interior partitions. . .'

Tara suppressed a yawn. She had been back in the Insco office for over a week, reviewing reports written by other inspectors. Normally, she quite enjoyed the work routine, but at the moment she just couldn't work up any interest in sprinkler systems and fire tanks and buckets of sand.

All her concentration seemed to have gone since the fire, together with all her joy in life.

'Construction rating: Class 1. Protection rating. . .'—oh, what the hell, Pete Norton was a skilled engineer, and if he said it was good, who was she to argue? She checked his rating in pencil and flicked over the page.

'I know I said I wanted those back PDQ, Tara, but I did mean you to read the damn things.'

Guiltily, she snapped to attention and brought her eyes up to meet Jim Backley's.

'I was doing, Jim. Honest.'

'Not that last page you didn't.'

'True,' she admitted. 'But I did read all the others.'

Jim's callused hand shot out and whipped Pete Norton's report from under her pencil. 'Where's this report for?' he fired at her.

'Er. . . Oh, Jim, I don't know. It's a warehouse

somewhere, light construction, reasonable sprinkler system, badly organised emergency team.'

'West Germany?'

'I guess so.'

'Rubbish. It's just outside Basingstoke.'

Tara sighed. 'Sorry, Jim.'

'You used to be one of my most reliable reviewers, Tara.'

'Is that a compliment?'

'Double-edged one.' Jim retrieved from the corner of her desk the pile of reports he had brought with him, and fanned them out across the desk in front of her. 'Honestly, kiddo. OK, most of these are so solid you'd barely need to change a thing, but Jeff Warden must have had a brainstorm when he checked this protection rating as excellent, and you haven't flagged it—and the couple of reports by that dumb girl I fired last week are crap from start to finish. You should have gone through every line of these calculations, they're riddled with errors, but you've barely caught a quarter of them.'

'What can I say? I'm sorry.'

'So am I. Hey, come in my office a minute.'

'Oh, God, Jim, you wouldn't——'

'Fire you? Too damn right I wouldn't. Now get your ass over here before I really lose my temper.'

Sheepishly, Tara followed Jim down through the main office and into his smaller office at the end of the corridor.

'OK,' he said, launching into his swivel chair, and swinging round to glance up at the assignment chart, then back at her. 'I let you off calling Hamilton, and you've had ten days to prove me right, and what have you done? Proved me wrong.'

'Oh, no,' Tara said in a failing voice.

'Oh, yes,' Jim said starkly. 'Tara, your love life's

none of my business, but your work is, and I can't let you carry on like this. We've tried the softly-softly treatment, and that doesn't work, so now it's time for the shock treatment. ECF Boulogne on Monday.'

'I'll resign.'

'No, you won't, Tara. You couldn't handle resigning at the moment. You need Insco, and we need you. Especially I need you, because I've got a line on Hamilton through you.'

'Jim, that's the last thing you've got.'

'Now look at it from Insco's perspective,' Jim said rationally, leaning forward across his desk, and fixing her with an intent, serious gaze. 'It's easy to skate over the human element in fire protection, but you've learned enough by now to know it's the most important aspect of all. No protection's truly automatic. Even the best-resourced system's got to be maintained and checked, backed up with a well-drilled fire team. . .'

'Spare me the lecture,' Tara said sharply.

'It won't be long. The thing is, those ECF plants aren't up to Insco standards—not only in physical protection, but in management attitudes, too. I don't care what Hamilton's like as a lover, but I do care what kind of security regime he runs, and I can tell you his is lousy at the moment. He's no fire protection fanatic, and nor are his security managers. And it's not only from your reports I've read that; it's in Jack Hughes' report on the Lyons factory, and half a dozen others too.'

'The fire at Louviers might stir things up,' Tara offered.

'It might—but I can't rely on mights, Tara. It's too easy for Hamilton and his staff to dismiss arson as a one-off, one crazy nutter getting back at them. They've got to get the message that it was poor protection which turned a small incident into a disaster. They've got to overhaul the fire precautions at every one of those plants, for their own sakes as much as ours. I'm putting every spare inspector I've got on to the remaining ECF inspections, till we've finished the lot and dumped the whole set of reports on Hamilton's desk—and I'm putting you on to Boulogne because it's the biggest plant, with the highest hazards. I want a solid inspection of every square inch of that joint. I want watertight recommendations checked twice over. Then I want you personally to fix an appointment with Hamilton, and slam the report down in front of him.'

'Oh, no.'

'Oh, yes. And I want you to come away from that meeting with a written commitment to deal with every recommendation within the next six months.'

'Six months!'

'All right, a year for any expenditure over a hundred thousand francs.'

'Jim, if you think he'll do that for me, you're——'

'He'll do it,' Jim said stubbornly.

Silence. Tara twisted her hands together, shuffled her feet, tried desperately to think of a way of getting out of this. Once he had made up his mind Jim Backley was about as movable as a bull elephant, though, and she couldn't come up with any bright ideas that would be likely to sway him.

'All right,' she said slowly, 'I'll do the inspection. But not the interview with Hamilton, Jim. Let me off that, please.'

Jim slowly shook his head. 'You can do it, Tara. You're stronger than you think. And I need you to do it, because whether it's love, or guilt, or anger, you get to the guy. Now you can't deny that,' he went on, overriding her protestations, 'because I know it's true.

So you go there, and you use every weapon you've got against him. You can fight your own personal battles or not, I don't mind—that's none of my business. But you fight Insco's battle, because that's your business *and* mine, and it's got to be done.'

'I'm the last person he'd listen to when it comes to fire protection.'

'Then you'd better be the best as well, hadn't you?' Jim shot back.

CHAPTER TEN

'So Jim's assigned you to do ECF Boulogne?' Jake Farmer, the American head of Insco's marketing department, remarked to Tara a couple of days later. 'Should be quite a job.'

'It's a complex factory,' Tara agreed.

'Complex business, plastics, especially these days.' He glanced down at her desk. 'You've been reading up the background?'

Tara flushed as he flicked open the marketing department's background file on ECF, which she had borrowed the day before. 'I thought it would be a help if I—I knew what the situation was like there.'

'It's tough,' Jake said tersely. 'That company was in bad shape when SHP took over. Add in the latest tranche of environmental regulations and the fire at Louviers, and Hamilton's got his back to the wall.'

The file fell open at a press-clipping from the *Financial Times* with a screaming headline, 'BANQUE DE FRANCE TO PULL THE PLUG ON ECF'.

'Do you. . .think it'll go under?' she asked nervously.

Jake, a wiry, powerful man, gave her a sideways glance. 'No,' he said shortly. 'That was a month ago.' He flicked the clipping over to reveal the next one, headlined 'HAMILTON FINALISES ECF RESCUE DEAL'. 'Brad Hamilton's a sharp guy; he'll pull through.'

So he would. She guessed he always would; he wasn't a loser.

But to come so close—and a month ago! That

discovery had horrified her when she'd begun to read through the file. A month ago she had been with Brad, in Rouen, and yet she had had no idea about the negotiations the paper described.

She had even met the bankers involved. She remembered it clearly; drinks in the boardroom, to which she had arrived late, and dinner in the Old Town afterwards. 'Charm them,' Brad had said. 'It's important.' And she had done her best, but she'd been tired from a long day's work, and there hadn't been time beforehand to ask him what the bankers were doing in Rouen.

Maybe Brad had always believed he'd pull through, but she knew now that he'd sweated all the same. And had she shared his worries? Not in the least; at the time she had been preoccupied with corroding sprinkler pipework at an electronics factory.

'You've met Hamilton?' Jake Farmer asked curiously, taking in her pale face.

'Yes.'

'I saw him in Rouen last week. He took the fire hard. Still, it's a good time to push him for better protection at the other locations.'

'He doesn't have the money, surely.'

Jake gave her a narrow look. 'That's his problem,' he said coolly. 'Hustling for good protection's your job. It's no use watering down your recommendations because you know ECF's in deep water. Cash in on the warehouse fire, and throw the book at them.' He paused. 'OK?'

'OK,' Tara agreed, in a faint voice.

'I'll take the file,' Jake went on, shutting it firmly, and tucking it under his arm. 'I see your thinking, but you're wrong, Tara. Your job is to be objective about the fire protection. Don't think about the wider issues; that's my patch.'

'Thanks for the lecture, Jake.'

'No sweat.' Jake's grin neatly defused her irony. 'Hey, you ever thought about transferring to marketing?'

'I can't say I have.'

'We'll have to talk about it some time. You've the talent. The work's hard, but the money's good—better than you're getting now.'

'I'll think about it.'

'Do that,' he agreed, gently cuffing her shoulder, then striding off down the office.

And she hadn't finished the file! she thought, with faint irritation. The file was fat; ECF was a big company, and it hit the headlines with monotonous regularity. But she'd got the gist of it, the soap opera the financial journalists had made out of 'millionaire whizz-kid' Brad Hamilton, riding into town like the cowboy she'd first taken him for, and taking on the baddies one by one.

She'd read that he'd hired temporary warehouse space near Rouen, and had announced plans to rebuild the Louviers warehouse. 'Statistics show,' he'd been quoted as saying in one clipping, 'that many companies never recover from a major fire. I can tell you, though, that ECF is going to be an exception to that rule.'

She had told him that. She had quoted those statistics to him, months before, in Montelimar.

At least now she wouldn't be able to waste any more time staring at a blurred newspaper photo of Brad, looking tall and severe, standing with Juliette at his side in front of the mangled steel frame and sodden ashes of the wrecked warehouse.

Her eyes dipped to the report she was reviewing, but the picture of Brad and Juliette was there in her mind, superimposed on Pete Norton's scrawl.

Juliette, of course, had known all about his problems. Juliette had been there all the time. Juliette was still there, at his side.

Jealousy stabbed into her at the thought, stiletto-sharp. What was worse, she knew it was her own fault that Juliette was with him, and she was not. Because Brad had been right; he'd needed her support, and she hadn't given it to him.

What had he said, back in Rouen? He'd come to her for a moment's respite, and all she had brought him were demands that he buy a fire pump.

She had blamed *him* for putting ECF before her, but it seemed to her now that he had just as much reason to blame her, for putting Insco before him. She had loved him, but not well enough. She hadn't wanted to be the kind of wife that he really needed. It was her own fault that she had lost him, and she knew it.

And now, thanks to Jim Backley's warped astuteness, she was supposed to muscle her way back into his still crisis-ridden company, and demand that he buy *more* fire pumps!

Damn Jim, she thought irritably; and damn Jake Farmer, too.

Though the air was cool, the sun shone as Tara collected her gate pass at ECF's Boulogne factory, and swung her hired Peugeot into the car park. Her eyes swept across the ranks of parked cars. No red Ferrari.

Of course not; Brad was surely in Rouen. But she felt sure he knew that she was coming to Boulogne, to ECF, and she had been psyched up to encounter him.

Two weeks of phoning, then silence. He obviously wasn't looking to see her any more. But why had he wanted to talk to her so badly in the days after the fire and their break-up—and why had he stopped wanting to? Had it simply been that he'd realised he'd wrongly accused her, and wanted to apologise?

It had to be that, she thought wearily. He couldn't ask her to try again at their relationship because he couldn't offer to compromise over the issue of her working. How could he? She understood now, as she hadn't before, that he literally *couldn't* compromise. He needed a wife who would give him the kind of support that a career-orientated woman simply couldn't manage to give.

And she was a career-orientated woman—except that now her job felt like an ordeal, and the only thing clear in her mind was her memory of Brad, and the ache whenever she thought of all she had lost.

The factory made expanded polystyrene products and, as Jim had warned Tara, it was huge and complex. She had been allocated five days to make her inspection and prepare a report.

On the second day—still without any word from Brad—she asked the general manager's secretary to ring the European director's office and fix her an appointment with him for the following Monday.

She half expected Brad to refuse to give her an appointment, instead passing her down to Michel Guerard or another member of his staff, but the general manager's secretary came back almost immediately, to tell her that four o'clock on Monday would suit Mr Hamilton.

So. She would see him, after all. She'd do her job and he'd do his. He'd apologise, she guessed, for his accusations. And that would be that.

Or would it?

There was still a gulf between them, and she knew he wouldn't—he couldn't—meet her part-way in an attempt to close it. But she still had the option of

closing it herself. She could tell him that she understood, now. She could tell him she knew what pressure
he had been under. She could tell him she appreciated
his need for a wife who would give him total support.
She could offer to become that wife.

All the sacrifices would be hers. It would be hard,
maybe even impossible, for her to cope with the kind
of life he was offering her. But it was hard—no, more
than hard, impossible—to go on living without him.
Wouldn't it be better to make that gesture, and to work
on making a success of a life with Brad?

Could she do it? Would he still want her to do it?
She didn't know, yet.

She worked on. The factory was very busy, since
Brad had ordered the management to step up production to help replace the stock lost at Louviers. Its
buildings were old, some of its machinery was out-
dated, and its sprinkler system was a tinpot affair that
should have been replaced twenty years earlier.

It needed new sprinkler pipework and a new fire
pump. It also needed new machines in the moulding
shop, and a decent office-block. And Brad needed to
pare costs to the bone, if ECF was to weather the long-
term effects of the fire, and to become a profitable
company.

Three months before, Tara would only have noticed
the first of those issues. She was used to judging
organisations by how willing their managers were to
carry out her recommendations, and nothing else about
them had really concerned her. But now, with ECF,
she couldn't help seeing the wider picture.

This was what Jake Farmer had warned her of. She
understood his warning, but it didn't cool her unease.

On Thursday, in the post, came a sheaf of Insco
reports on other ECF locations, for her to present to

Brad together with her own recommendations. She flicked through them, and reckoned up the cost of the work Insco required done. It added up to hundreds of thousands of dollars—more, she knew, than the company in its current state could conceivably afford.

She finished her inspection on Friday afternoon, and stayed in Boulogne on Saturday and Sunday, writing up her report and thinking. Then, on Monday, she got up early, read her report over, and dressed in the brown suit and lilac blouse she had worn when she'd first met Brad, four months earlier.

She washed her hair, and brushed it out in a soft cloud before tying it back in her usual pony-tail. She made-up her face with shaking, but determined hands. Then she checked out of her hotel, and drove down to Rouen, to the ECF Headquarters building.

She parked in the familiar underground car park. It was only half-past three. A great ball of apprehension seemed to have gathered in her stomach, and there was a sour taste in her mouth.

She didn't take the express lift straight away, instead walking back up the curving ramp, and out on to the street. She walked rapidly, almost at random, until she came to the river. She crossed the road, and walked a few yards downstream to the Pont Jeanne d'Arc. In the middle of the bridge she stopped, looking down at the water.

The weather had improved again, and by October standards it was an exceptionally fine day. Sunlight sparkled on the water, and the trees were just beginning to turn to their autumn colours.

One summer, that was all she and Brad had had. One summer had forged and destroyed their relationship.

The briefcase with the reports was heavy in her hand.

In a few minutes she would have to do as Jim and Jake expected her to do—present those reports to Brad, and pile on the pressure to make him spend money that ECF couldn't afford on fire protection.

This would be the last time they would meet, and then they would part forever, with Brad still believing that she was an obsessed virago who cared more about sprinkler systems than she did about the man she loved.

But she wasn't! She didn't.

For a moment she had an insane desire to throw her briefcase out into the brownish waters of the Seine.

Common sense quashed the impulse almost immediately. The information in those reports was valuable, to Brad as well as to Insco. Good fire protection was vital, as the incident at Louviers had dramatically proved. But spending money on that protection was only one of Brad's priorities, and she wished she could find a way of showing him that she understood that, without failing in her obligations to Jim and Insco.

There wasn't a way, though. Insco's instructions were clear and pitiless. If she was choosing her career, choosing Insco, then she would have to follow her orders and demand that he agree to comply with all Insco's recommendations.

If she was choosing her career. . .

Let me just see him, she thought, yearningly. Let me just come face to face with him, and look in his eyes. Then I'll know how he feels—and then I'll know what I should do.

She turned her back on the river, returned to the shore, and made her way slowly to the tall glass doors of the ECF building.

The receptionist recognised her, and smiled. Tara gave a wan smile back. She took the private express lift, was hurtled upwards, then emerged on to the top floor, coming face to face with an icy-looking Juliette.

'Hello, Juliette,' Tara said quietly.

Juliette rose to her feet and took a couple of steps towards her. 'You bitch,' she hissed.

A sharp indrawn breath was Tara's only response.

'Coming back now,' Juliette went on, still in a hissing whisper, 'after all the harm you did. I don't know how you have the gall.'

'It's my job,' Tara said unsteadily.

'Huh! You could have cried off. Insco's got other inspectors. It didn't have to be you who came.'

Juliette took another step towards Tara. They were within touching distance now, the Frenchwoman towering over the slight English girl.

'You think you'll get him back, don't you?' Juliette whispered accusingly. 'That's why you've really come. Well, you won't. He's mine now. Do you hear me? He's mine.'

The blood drained from Tara's body. She swayed under the force of Juliette's attack and the shock of her words.

She hadn't dared to face up to this possibility, but she knew, instinctively, that it had always been there. In the cutting. The picture, Brad and Juliette together amid the wreckage of the fire. Juliette had been there all along, waiting to pounce if she ever loosed her hold on Brad. This was what she had dreaded since she had first met Brad's assistant. And now it had happened.

'He doesn't want a woman like you,' Juliette said insistently. 'You're no good for him. You hurt him, you bitch, and now just when he's got over it you have to come back again. I'm not having it. You're not seeing him. You can give your papers to me, I'll give them to him.'

'No, I. . . I. . .'

Tara's voice faltered into silence.

Juliette was so horribly right. She hadn't come to present Insco's recommendations. She had come because of Brad, because she ached to see him again, to be with him, to touch him, to love him. Jim's orders had been an excuse—a ghastly, inappropriate excuse— but not the reason for her to come, any more than Insco was the reason for her to go on living. It was Brad who was that reason.

From the moment Jim had given her his order, her mind had been full of this meeting with Brad. Nothing else had mattered. Not his mistrust, not her own selfish desire for fulfilment through her career. The only thing that mattered was that she couldn't endure life without him, and would give anything, *anything*, to be back in his arms.

But now she could make all her sacrifices, and they would be in vain. Brad hadn't given her the time to discover her true priorities. Just when she was on the verge of giving up everything for him, he had given her up—for a bitchy, elegant blonde.

'Give them to me,' Juliette went on, in a fierce whisper. 'Give them to me and go.'

'I can't. . . I don't. . .'

At that moment the door to Brad's office opened.

Tara flinched. She couldn't see him, not now. She couldn't bear it. Even as the dark bulk of his body emerged from behind the heavy door, she turned, panicking, to the lift.

The doors were shut, but the lift was still waiting on that floor, and they opened immediately she pushed the button.

'Tara!' Brad called, somewhere behind her. 'Tara, what are you——'

The lift doors closed, cutting off his words.

She pressed the ground floor button instinctively, and leaned against the cold metal side of the lift. The lift fell rapidly, taking her away from him. Away from the pain, the unendurable pain, into a duller and deeper agony, which would never end.

The lift jerked to a halt, and the doors opened on to the foyer, with its orange carpet, and its plants, and its chic receptionists.

Oh. She should have pressed the basement button, for the car park. She. . .

No, she couldn't drive off, not yet. She couldn't face getting into her car; she would feel trapped inside it. She was going to be sick, really sick.

Blindly she rushed for the doors, and out on to the road. This time she ran in the other direction, towards the Old Town.

'Tara!' The shout came from behind her. She ran faster, faster, but her legs were short, and she was hampered by her heavy briefcase. Before she could lose herself in the narrow streets around the Rue du Gros Horloge, Brad's hand had caught and trapped her arm.

She shuddered to a halt, panting, frantic, her eyes looking everywhere but at him, although she was acutely conscious not only of his grip, but also of the nearness of his body, and the hot aura that emanated from him.

'For heaven's sake, Tara. What caused that?'

'I. . . I. . .' She pulled her arm, hard, but failed to loosen his grip. He swung her round, grabbing her other wrist, and she sighed in pain and frustration, her eyes cast downwards.

'You wouldn't understand,' she said, in a faltering voice.

'No, I wouldn't,' Brad said grimly. 'Come back. Please.'

She shivered. He surely couldn't fail to understand how she felt, how terrible this was for her. And perhaps he did understand to some extent, because he added, in a gentler voice, 'All right, we won't go back yet. We'll get a coffee somewhere. There must be a. . .here,' he finished, dragging her along the pavement until they came to a small café. He pulled out one of the white-painted chairs, nudged her down into it, and still with his grip firm on one wrist, claimed a second chair for himself.

Tara fixed her eyes on the table-top, though the temptation to look properly at him was almost unbearable.

'Was it so hard to see me again?' he asked, in an oddly gruff voice.

'It was. . .' Tara's voice faded away. This was embarrassing, humiliating, a thousand times worse than she had feared. He surely knew how intensely he was affecting her, knew how vulnerable she was to him. But he couldn't expect her to put her feelings into words, now that he'd removed all hope of a happy ending.

'It's I who should be feeling bad about it,' Brad said harshly. 'Tara, when I think of the things I said, during the fire. . . Believe me, I didn't mean it. Even then, I didn't honestly believe you'd done it. I tried to phone you afterwards, to tell you that. You do believe me, don't you? I was tired and worried and I said what I knew would wound you, but I knew all along that you'd never have been capable of starting the fire.'

Tara stared downwards. Down below the table-top, to her arm, to her hand, to her wrist encircled by his

big brown hand. To his steel wristwatch, his suit
trousers, his shiny black shoes.

So it was true. He'd phoned only to tell her that he
knew he'd made a mistake with the accusation. Then
he'd turned to Juliette—when? Perhaps even at
Louviers, when that photograph had been taken.

'You do believe me?' Brad went on insistently. 'Tell
me you believe me. Tell me you forgive me, please,
Tara.'

'I forgive you,' she said slowly.

'I was a fool, and I know it.'

'No!' The bitterness in his voice caught at her and,
instinctively, forgetting her resolutions, she raised her
eyes to his. To his face, strong-jawed, shadowed with
exhaustion, slightly hollow-eyed.

Jake Farmer had been right. He'd taken the fire
hard. And there was an odd compassion in her voice as
she went on, 'No, Brad, you were never that.'

'Of course I was,' he said grimly, his dark eyes fixed
firmly on hers. 'I was a fool all the time, too harassed
to listen to you, or to consider your viewpoint. Even
over the fire protection, although you were proved so
terribly right about the danger.'

'That's true,' she admitted. Then she took a deep
breath, and pulled her hand free. He released it this
time, almost to her surprise. 'Anyway, you're forgiven.'
Her body heavy with despair, she got to her feet. 'I
brought some reports,' she added, her voice tight and
barely controlled. 'On Boulogne and some of the other
locations. I'll leave them with you. There's a heap of
recommendations, but——'

Her voice caught, then she went on, determinedly,
'I'm supposed to get your commitment to comply with
them all, but I'm not going to do it.' Fingers fumbling,
she unfastened the catches of her briefcase, and fished

out the sheaf of reports. She dropped them on the café table. 'ECF can't afford better fire protection; I know that now. I've had to recommend new equipment at Boulogne, but I—well, I don't expect you to put it in.'

'Tara, what is this? What are you saying?'

She wrenched her eyes from his for the final time. 'Goodbye,' she said on a sob. 'Just—goodbye.'

'Sit down!'

'Brad, please. Let me——'

'No.' He stood, abruptly, took the briefcase out of her hand and tossed it to the ground. His hands trapped hers, firm and insistent. 'I haven't finished yet. I've got to talk to you. And I don't mean about those reports, though for heaven's sake, I know as well as you do that I've got to work on the fire protection after what happened at Louviers. I mean we've got to talk about us, Tara—you and me.'

'But there is no us any more.'

'And that's my fault,' Brad soberly agreed. 'Tara, I know it's going to take more than one apology before you truly forgive me, but you just said you did, and that's a start. Or didn't you mean it?'

'Of course I did!' She turned tear-filled eyes up to his. 'But Brad—please don't push me, because I can't bear it!'

'Just tell me one thing. Were these damned reports the only reason why you came?'

'Why else should I have come?' she faltered back.

'You have to ask me that?' His voice was incredulous. 'After all we were to each other?'

'But you. . .but Juliette. . .'

'Juliette? What's Juliette got to do with this?'

'She told me you. . .that you and she. . .'

'Never!' Brad exclaimed roughly. 'Tara, you surely

don't believe that! I haven't looked at another woman since the day I met you!'

His voice was thick with incredulity. She couldn't help but believe him, although she gave in to the temptation to ask, 'Really?'

'Swear to God. I don't know what she told you, Tara, but she's nothing more to me than a competent assistant, and never has been.'

'Even after the fire?'

'After the fire? Tara, after the fire I was *distraught*,' he said insistently. 'Thinking I'd lost you, lost ECF— the last thing I wanted was to console myself with that frigid female! And it's the last thing I want now. There's only one thing I want now, Tara, and that's to find us a way forward.'

'Me too,' she said fervently. 'Brad, I've been stupid too. I never thought about how it was for you, taking on that huge job in a strange country. You said you needed support, but I never really understood how much you needed it. I was so scared of losing my own identity, being submerged by you and ECF. It was only after I'd left that I realised how much you needed from me, that I hadn't been able to give.'

'I needed you.' His hand slid down her wrist to wrap around hers. 'That was all, Tara. I needed you.'

'Full time,' she added, with a rueful note.

'No. Not really.' He urged her to sit again, and paused for long enough to order two brandies from the hovering, and very curious, waiter. Then, 'Tara,' he went on, 'I've thought about it a lot since Louviers, and I've come to understand your position, too. Adrienne and I went so wrong, and one problem with the two of us was that I was trying so hard not to have us fall into the same traps. I do need support and

reassurance—who doesn't?—but I'm neither so inse-
cure, nor such an egomaniac, as to make that a full-
time job!'

'But I should have learned more. About ECF, and
your problems, and——'

'No,' he said firmly. 'I'm not looking to come home
each night and pour my heart out about work! Even
over the past few months, when I've been under a hell
of a lot of pressure, I didn't really want that. It'd be
enough if I felt secure in your love, if I could know you
were always there for me.'

'I do love you, Brad. And I *will* always be there.
Even though that means not travelling, and——'

'Not necessarily,' he interrupted. 'It's a counsel of
perfection, maybe, to find you waiting for me at home
every evening, but it's not one that I'd want to cost you
your career. I was wrong about that, Tara. I've always
loved your independence and your strong mind, and
the last thing I really want to do is to curb it.'

'You mean. . .'

'I mean, my love, that I want you back. On your
terms.'

'But I was willing to come back on *your* terms!'

'You were?' His face, first incredulous, slowly light-
ened into a look of sheer joy. 'What fools we've been.'

'Oh, Brad.'

'Oh——' Brad turned to the waiter, who had
returned with their brandies. 'We ought to make that
champagne,' he murmured drily.

'We ought to be working.'

'Damn work!' Brad cheerfully ordered a bottle of
champagne from the waiter, pushed a brandy across to
her, then said, 'We work too hard, both of us. You
were right about that, darling; in some ways I did put
ECF first, but that's not really how I want my life to

be. When you made those accusations, I guess I reacted so badly largely because I knew you were right. I never let myself be objective about SHP. I hated joining that company more than I ever admitted to myself. I hated throwing up my painting, acknowledging that I'd been a failure——'

'But you weren't!'

'Not entirely,' he agreed with a rueful smile. 'But I had to make myself think I was one, or I couldn't have borne to put it all behind me. I had to stop painting completely for the same reason, and I threw myself into work at SHP because that was the only way I could endure the situation. I had to prove I'd been right to make the switch. I had to be the best manager ever. But I pushed myself too hard sometimes, and I never gave myself enough of a chance to relax.'

'I saw that,' Tara agreed. 'That painting, Brad, over your bed——'

'The one in the café? You don't know how often I took down that painting, or how often I hung it up again. It was a reminder of a different me, the person I'd left behind. I hated it, and yet I knew I needed it there.'

'You need to be like that,' Tara suggested.

'Sometimes I do,' he agreed. 'Like this afternoon. I'll call Juliette from here, and tell her I won't be back. There's work, sure, but there's nothing that can't wait until tomorrow. Today my priority's you—and us.'

He was as good as his word, making the phone-call immediately, and by the time he returned the waiter had brought their champagne. Brad opened it himself, and his weary face was transformed by delight as he raised his glass to Tara's.

'We should do this often,' he said gaily. 'I'll try to

relax more in future, and get a better perspective on things.'

'I won't take that promise too seriously,' Tara teased. She knew he was too used to his pressurised life, and the demands on him were too intense, for him to make overnight changes in his lifestyle.

'No, really; I ought to delegate more. To you, not least, if you can be persuaded to work for ECF. I've thought about your suggestion a lot, and I like it. I was too angry when you made it to take it seriously, but I can see now that you were right. I haven't put enough resources into security—or at least, ECF hasn't.'

'I'd like that,' Tara agreed. 'I don't want to be the little woman sitting at home; I'd much rather play a real part in your organisation.'

'You will,' he assured her. 'And now, my love, we'll take a taxi home, since this champagne has gone straight to my head, and then we'll celebrate our reunion properly.'

'You mean this isn't proper?'

'What I have in mind is something much more intimate.' He pulled her to her feet, then went on to draw her body into the long lean length of his, and bring his mouth down on hers.

Tara's senses reeled. It was weeks since she had touched him, and his kiss now was like water on quicklime. It hissed through her body, making her intensely aware of the feel of his body through his formal business-suit, of the familiar evocative scent of him, of the desire that was already gathering strength within her.

'Marry me tomorrow,' he breathed, when he reluctantly released her.

'I'd marry you this minute.'

Brad smiled down into her eyes. 'In my heart,' he murmured, 'you just did.'

CHAPTER ELEVEN

'Now it gives me great pleasure to announce that this warehouse is formally open.'

The tall, rangy man paused a moment, drinking in the applause that had greeted his short speech. Then he tugged on the cord attached to the little pair of curtains, drawing them open to reveal a small engraved plaque.

Tara leaned forward from where she stood, next to Brad at one side of the plaque, and read the inscription. It was only short, giving the date that the old warehouse had burned down, the date of this ceremoney to open its replacement, and the name of the man who had performed it, Francis J. Hamilton.

'Now for the serious business,' Mr Hamilton went on, in a lighter voice. 'Honey, where's the champagne?'

'Here, darling,' his wife assured him, approaching with the first bottle just as a waitress appeared with a tray of empty glasses. Frank Hamilton took the bottle from her, then paused, looked around, and let his eyes rest on Brad.

'I guess this is your department, son.'

'Sure should be; I've had plenty of practice recently,' Brad agreed, laughing as he moved to his father's side. He ripped off the foil and loosened the wire cage over the cork with easy expertise. Then came the satisfying pfft! of the cork erupting, and the chattering and laughter as the glasses were filled and handed around the small assembly.

Tara seemed to spend more time clinking her glass in toasts than in drinking its contents as she circulated among the guests, thanking them for their good wishes. It was only a fortnight since she and Brad had returned from their Caribbean honeymoon, so this was the first opportunity many people had had to congratulate them on their marriage.

Jim Backley was among them, and very complacent he looked too, for a man who had just lost one of his best fire protection engineers—as she teasingly told him.

'It's not all to my disadvantage, Tara,' he assured her. 'If you bring all ECF's locations up to the protection standards of this one, then I'll have nothing to complain about.'

'Except the size of Insco's premiums,' she shot back. 'And to be fair, neither you nor I will get that done overnight. My budget's tight, and I'll have to concentrate on tightening up fire teams and housekeeping for a while, leaving the more expensive recommendations on ice.'

'But you're still glad you took the corporate security manager job?'

'Very glad,' she said simply. 'And not only because I'll be working with Brad. I didn't like always making recommendations and then moving on before anything was done about them; it's good to think I'll be responsible for really making things happen this time around. And I'll be glad to travel a bit less, too.'

'Looking forward to a family?'

'In a year or two, we hope,' she agreed, glancing across at her husband—and connecting instead with Frank Hamilton, who had evidently heard their last exchange while he was approaching.

'Ah, that's important,' he said heartily. 'We need to line up the next generation to take over the family firm.'

'You never know, Frank. They might turn out to want to be artists instead.'

'Think I've heard that one somewhere before,' Frank said with a harsh laugh. 'I must say this, though. When Brad threw up his painting and came back to the States, both Mary and I asked ourselves whether we'd leaned on him too hard; but he's turned out a damn sight better manager than he ever was a painter.'

'He's a very good painter,' Tara said loyally—and with conviction.

'He's a very good manager too,' Jim put in.

'That he is. In fact, all told, he's about the finest son a man could ask for.'

'He's a pretty good husband as well,' Tara murmured, half under her breath, as Brad too crossed to join the group.

He grinned at her, and bent down to whisper in her ear. 'What makes me think my ears ought to be burning?'

'Tell you later,' she whispered back.

He didn't push for an answer. His teeth just nipped the top of her ear, then he straightened up in time to listen to what his father was saying.

'I was just telling Jim here about the German deal.'

'Vorplas? Yeah, it's all signed now, and we'll be announcing the acquisition in a couple of days.'

'That should keep you busy,' Jim commented.

'Not too busy,' Frank Hamilton amended. 'Brad's got his priorities right, and he believes in life outside work, especially at the moment! I wanted to stretch him, as well as to take advantage of a good business opportunity, but it was his idea that we put in separate managers for ECF and for Vorplas, reporting to him.'

'Sounds wise.'

'It's a long-term strategy. I'm feeling so good these days, I'm reckoning to carry on for another six or seven years. The last thing I want's my son queuing up to step into my shoes before I'm good and ready to quit 'em.'

'I wouldn't do that, Dad,' Brad said reassuringly. 'Anyway, I reckon Tara and I will be pretty happy in Europe.'

'So do I,' Tara agreed.

Brad held her eyes and smiled, and she knew that he was sharing her thoughts.

It wouldn't all be plain sailing. Running ECF had been a tough enough job, and the new reshuffle gave him no sinecure. But Brad was growing in confidence and skill, and she knew he'd enjoy the challenge of keeping abreast of the company's expansion and his father's expectations.

He'd never be a painter again—he'd made his last career choice. But he was more than content with his lot in life—and so was she, with hers.

'How about you, Tara?' Jim asked. 'It's not just Brad that this will affect; you will be taking on responsibility for Vorplas as well?'

Tara, her eyes still on Brad, gave a slow smile. He'd lived up to his promise to let her pursue her own career, but battles like hers weren't won overnight, and they still had to tread carefully, to keep a balance between her ambitions for herself and his need for her support, her longing for freedom and his desire to protect her. It was worth it, though, and together they were developing a pattern of give-and-take that promised to serve them well throughout their marriage.

'Not yet,' she said lightly. 'But we're keeping the situation under review.'

Brad burst into laughter. 'What this little scrap means,' he added, 'is that she's standing up to me again—and likely to win!'

Accept 4 Free Romances and 2 Free gifts

•FROM READER SERVICE•

An irresistible invitation from Mills & Boon Reader Service. Please accept our offer of 4 free Romances, a CUDDLY TEDDY and a special MYSTERY GIFT... Then, if you choose, go on to enjoy 6 captivating Romances every month for just £1.60 each, postage and packing free. Plus our FREE newsletter with author news, competitions and much more.

**Send the coupon below to:
Reader Service, FREEPOST, PO Box 236, Croydon, Surrey CR9 9EL.**

NO STAMP REQUIRED

Yes! Please rush me my 4 free Romances and 2 free gifts! Please also reserve me a Reader Service Subscription. If I decide to subscribe I can look forward to receiving 6 new Romances each month for just £9.60, postage and packing is free. If I choose not to subscribe I shall write to you within 10 days - I can keep the books and gifts whatever I decide. I may cancel or suspend my subscription at any time. I am over 18 of age.

Name Mrs/Miss/Ms/Mr _____ EP17R

Address _____

_____

Postcode _____ Signature _____

Mills & Boon

Next month's Romances

Each month, you can choose from a world of variety in romance with Mills & Boon. These are the new titles to look out for next month.

TEMPESTUOUS REUNION Lynne Graham

A CURE FOR LOVE Penny Jordan

UNDERCOVER AFFAIR Lilian Peake

GHOST OF THE PAST Sally Wentworth

ISTANBUL AFFAIR Joanna Mansell

ROARKE'S KINGDOM Sandra Marton

WHEN LOVE RETURNS Vanessa Grant

DANGEROUS INFATUATION Stephanie Howard

LETHAL ATTRACTION Rebecca King

STORMY RELATIONSHIP Margaret Mayo

HONG KONG HONEYMOON Lee Wilkinson

CONTRACT TO LOVE Kate Proctor

WINTER DESTINY Grace Green

AFRICAN ASSIGNMENT Carol Gregor

THE CHALK LINE Kate Walker

STARSIGN

HUNTED HEART Kristy McCallum